THE RAPTORS

Ray Hogan

CHIVERS

British Library Cataloguing in Publication Data available

This Large Print edition published by AudioGO Ltd, Bath, 2013.
Published by arrangement with Golden West Literary Agency

U.K. Hardcover   ISBN   978 1 4713 1122 2
U.K. Softcover   ISBN   978 1 4713 1123 9

Copyright © 1979 Ray Hogan
Copyright © 1980 by Ray Hogan in the British Commonwealth

Printed and bound in Great Britain by
MPG Books Group Limited

. . . for my wife, Lois, a wondrous lady beyond compare . . .

1

Off to the left on a mound of barren ground, a prairie dog broke the stillness with its sharp, querulous bark. Mungor twisted on his saddle, threw his glance into that direction, and then settled back.

He could not see the island of sun-bleached earth because of the pines, standing thick and tall around him and his two partners, sitting quietly nearby on their horses, but he remembered seeing the dog village as they rode in and had made mental note to avoid it if it became necessary to leave in a hurry; a running horse stepping in a prairie-dog hole was guaranteed a broken leg.

"What's taking them so long?"

Sonny King's voice was taut, strained, as he shifted his slight frame impatiently.

"Keep your shirt on," Mungor snapped curtly. "Waiting's part of the business." He paused, brushed the battered army campaign hat he was wearing to the back of his head, settled his attention on the remaining man. "And we're doing it without any shooting, Larch. You hear that?"

Oliver Larch, clad in a long, gray, concealing slicker, as were Mungor and Sonny, nodded woodenly. A dark, sullen man in his forties, he had small, unblinking eyes set deep in a round, stubble-covered face, little if any neck, and thick, powerful shoulders. He wasn't long out of prison and its mark lay upon him like a livid scar.

"I reckon I'll do what has to be done," he muttered and then added, "This sure better pan out, Mungor, else I'm riding on."

"It'll work," Mungor replied evenly, his eyes now on the office of the mining company, some hundred yards or so ahead through the trees and brush. The two men, couriers from the bank in Jaxon City, were still inside the small structure. Mungor could not see what was taking place but like as not they had completed their job of delivering the payroll, were now having themselves a cup of coffee and passing the time of day. They wouldn't tarry long, for they had a lengthy ride facing them, and once they had taken their leave, the moment to move in would be at hand.

Mungor had plotted it all carefully, knowing that he could afford to make no mistakes on this first venture if he was to keep Sonny and Larch as partners for the rest of his scheme — one designed to make rich men of them all.

They had arrived at the site of the Consolidated Gold Mine Company, deep in the Dakota Black Hills, three days earlier. Going alone, Mungor had visited the office of the concern, ostensibly in search of work, and while there had taken note of all things important — the safe that stood inside a closetlike compartment but whose heavy, iron door stood open during business hours, the number of men on the premises, the location of the back door, the barred windows, and the distance of the building from the mine shaft's entrance.

This information, added to the knowledge that the company always paid off its employees on the first of the month and thus had a large supply of cash on hand the day preceding, had simplified matters; robbing the place would be a cinch — if Larch and Sonny kept their heads.

And it would be the biggest and boldest job he had ever pulled — but he was ready. Ever since the war ended, bringing a close to his own personal world as well, he had knocked about the country indifferently seeking work and, finding none to his taste, had turned to petty outlawry as a means for staying alive.

He had learned much during those bitter years and now he knew what he wanted and just how to go about getting it. This was to be the initial step, the beginning, and when the campaign was over he, with Larch and Sonny, would be more than a thousand miles away, rich and enjoying the good life to which he felt he was justly entitled.

But they'd not be doing so together. Dave Mungor had no wish to associate with either of his partners any longer than would be necessary. Sonny, with a penchant for dousing himself with lilac water, was no more than twenty years of age and had but one thing besides plenty of money on his mind — women. He lived from one woman to the next, thinking of little if anything else but the pleasure he found in their company.

Such, undoubtedly, was due partly to the charm he exuded and partly to his looks; slender, with dark curling hair, blue eyes, and boyish features, he had a reckless sort of way about him that appealed to young girls and grown women alike — and he made the best of it. The chances were Sonny would spend his share of the money they gathered, however much, within the first year.

Larch was something else. A brutal, heavy-handed man with a background of criminal activity, his interest lay not with women, but in whiskey. He was never without a bottle from which he nipped continually, yet Mungor had yet to see the liquor have any effect upon him. It was as if he'd drunk so much in his lifetime that alcohol no longer had any effect upon his senses.

But he was a man Mungor wanted at his side, just as was Sonny. Both were expert with the pistols they wore, were totally unfamiliar with fear, and he felt that if he could keep them in line, and following his direction, all would work out fine.

The prairie dog barked again, and high above the trees in the late summer sky a score of vultures was soaring effortlessly in a broad circle as they centered their attention on something below. Two men appeared in the clearing that fronted the mining company office, coming from the shaft. They paused, glanced about, and entered.

Mungor frowned. That increased the odds if they remained. Ordinarily there were but three employees in attendance — but he'd not allow it to make any difference; three or five, they'd go through with the plan. He did wish, however, that the couriers from Jaxon City would pull out. It was growing late and other men, finished work for the day, would be emerging from the mine.

"What about them two?" Larch asked in his low, grating voice.

"What about them?" Mungor demanded irritably. "Changes nothing far as I'm concerned."

"Makes five of them in there — maybe even more, and you're saying we ain't to use no guns."

"Still saying it. Robbery's one thing — the law don't spend much time running down holdup men. Usually forget all about them in a few days. But killing — murder's something else. They don't give up on killers — you know that, Larch. They stay on the trail till they've tracked a man down and that's something we sure don't want — a half a dozen lawmen dogging our heels. Best we —"

Mungor's voice broke off as the two couriers came out of the mine office and crossed to the hitch rack. They stood there for several moments bantering with someone in the building and then, mounting up, wheeled about and rode off through the pines.

"Pull your masks up," Mungor said, drawing his bandanna into place across the lower half of his face. "You both know how this's to be done — what your job is. Do it right and we're on the road to riches. Let's go."

2

Mungor had brought his scheme into its final stages earlier in a Virginia City, Montana, saloon. He had, previous to then, laid his basic plans, known exactly what he intended to do, and lacked only the partners he felt were necessary to make it all possible.

Slumped in a chair at the end of the Yellow Cat's plank counter, he had watched the two men who he'd had his eye on for some time — a middle-aged hardcase named Ollie Larch, who, according to the barkeep, was not long out of prison, and a lean, hungry-looking kid called Sonny who sided him.

The latter, possibly, was too young, but Larch appeared to be just what he needed — a cool, quick-handed gunman who knew the ropes and could undoubtedly be depended upon in any situation. Mungor had then made a few discreet inquiries, learned nothing that refuted his assumptions other than the fact that Larch was something of a drinker; Sonny, however, who was much too handsome for his own good, he found had a weakness for women and thought of little else.

Mungor decided to forget him, make a deal with Larch, and find someone else for the third man, but when he broached the idea of a partnership to Larch and to him alone, the thick-shouldered man had turned it down flat. Sonny was a pal of his, had done him a good turn, and unless the boy could be in on whatever Mungor had in mind, he was not interested, no matter how good a proposition it was.

Sonny would be all right, Larch had assured Mungor. A bit wild when it came to women, he would admit, but that was a harmless pastime. When it came down to serious business Sonny could be relied on. The two of them had been in a few fights together and Larch said he couldn't have had a better man standing with him.

"All right," Mungor had said then, "I'm taking your word on it — and your guarantee —"

"The hell you are," Larch had cut in sourly. "I ain't guaranteeing nothing — nobody — not even my own brother, did I have one. You take Sonny on his own, or forget it."

"Just what I'm inclined to do," Mungor had said, suddenly weary of Larch's attitude. "What I'm offering's plenty — something that'll mean big money —"

"Don't you fret none about me, mister," Sonny had said. "When the shooting time comes I'll be right up there beside you and Larch, doing my part. Far as women are concerned, I ain't never seen one I couldn't handle, and you never will. Anyways, what I do when I ain't working is my business."

Mungor had considered that along with Ollie Larch's words and relented. He had been unable to find anyone in Virginia City who seemed to fill the bill as well as Larch, and he reckoned if he had to take Sonny to get the gunman, then that's what he would do. Like as not the boy would work out all right. If he didn't, well, somehow he'd manage to put the finger on Larch and make him responsible for the boy.

"Now, just what's all this big deal you're so all-fired proud of about?" Sonny had asked when the matter was settled and they sat down at a table in the rear of the saloon.

Mungor set the bottle and glasses he had obtained at the bar in front of them, studied each man thoughtfully. "How'd you like to get rich?"

Sonny grinned, flung a glance at one of the saloon girls passing nearby, and nodded. Larch shrugged.

"Who wouldn't?" he muttered, pouring himself a drink.

Over in the far side of the room a fight between two cowhands had broken out. Yells went up amid the crashing sounds of chairs and tables going over and being trampled underfoot. Sonny sprang erect, starting to hurry off toward the confusion.

"Sit down," Mungor ordered in a quiet, firm voice. "What I've got to say is a damn sight more important than that ruckus."

Sonny frowned, settled back on his chair. "Now, maybe I ain't all that interested in whatever you're aiming to talk about —"

"You will be," Mungor said, "unless fifteen or maybe twenty thousand dollars don't mean anything to you."

The younger man whistled softly. Larch's thick brows lifted. "Apiece?"

"Apiece," Mungor said.

The gunman wagged his head, toyed with the glass of whiskey held between a thumb and forefinger. "That's a hell of a lot of money. What are you figuring to do — bust open the U.S. mint?"

Mungor permitted himself a slow smile. A

17

tall man who still maintained the military bearing acquired during the war, he was just past thirty, had pale, expressionless eyes, thick brown hair, and a decidedly square jaw. He wore a full mustache, was letting a beard take over the lower half of his face.

He was clothed in the remains of his army uniform — hat, trousers, coat, and boots, but the shirt had long since given out and had been replaced by one purchased at some time during his wanderings.

"A man'd be a fool to try that," he said. "Even if he pulled it off, the federal marshals would never quit looking for him. What I've mapped out's not only safer but easier."

"Then where we going to find that much money?" Sonny demanded, now thoroughly interested. "Must figure fifty, sixty thousand dollars!"

"A dozen, maybe two dozen different places, all the way from here — or I reckon I ought to say the Black Hills — to Mexico."

Larch refilled his glass, settled back to give that thought. Sonny drew a small bottle of barber's lilac water from a pocket in his jacket and absently rubbed a bit on his jaw.

"It's taken me close to a year to get this plan set up," Mungor said. "I've figured every detail and I know it'll work — and pay off big. Only one thing you maybe won't like."

"What's that?" Larch asked.

"We get done with it, it'll mean living in Mexico — at least for a couple of years till it all blows over."

"Ain't nothing wrong with that!" Sonny said with a wide, captivating smile. "Been told them Mexican señoritas are really something!"

"With the kind of money we'll wind up with, a man will be able to live like a king down there," Mungor said, ignoring Sonny's comment.

"For a fact," Larch agreed. "I'd not be thinking about leaving. I'd stay put, right there."

"Way I look at it, too," Mungor said, pleased there had been no objections to what some men might have considered a drawback.

"When do we start this here shindig — and where?" Sonny wondered, eyes again on one of the girls crossing the room to the stairs that led up to the second floor. "I got a little unfinished business I'm honing to attend to."

"You'll have time," Mungor replied. "I figure we best head out in the morning for Dakota — the Black Hills. Gold mine up there that's first on my list."

"Gold mine!" Larch echoed in disgust. "How in the hell are we going to rob a gold mine?"

"Not robbing the mine — we're grabbing the payroll. Ought to be worth five or six thousand dollars. We slip in quiet — got to move now because it's getting close to the end of the month and paying-off time — take the money and ride out, fast.

"From then on it's hit and run — a bank or maybe a big general store, or a gambling house. I've got a list, like I've said, of the places where there'll be plenty of cash. Big thing is we keep moving — hit and run. We travel light and fast — and we change horses, buying them and not stealing them — ever so often so's we always have good animals under us and so's nobody'll be able to identify us by what we're riding.

"We'll keep working south, heading toward the Mexican border all the time. It's a good thousand miles from here, and that gives us a lot of room to do our moving around in —"

"And get caught in," Larch grumbled with a shake of his head.

"Long as we're careful and use our heads — and keep going, nobody'll get caught. That's the secret of it: hit the place quick and get out of town fast."

"That part's fine, but I'm telling you this right now, I ain't never letting myself get boxed in. I see it coming, I'll pull out, leave you flat."

Mungor considered the gunman narrowly. "I never figured you for a man who'd back off," he said. He was surprised, had thought Ollie Larch was one man who'd never turn tail under any circumstance.

"I ain't caring what you figured. Boils down to this — nobody ain't ever caging me again. I've spent all the time I aim to behind bars, and if the odds stack up against me and it's that or run — I'm running."

There were a few moments of quiet following Larch's declaration during which Mungor studied the backs of his folded hands. The saloon had settled back to normalcy, the disturbance on the far side of the room having ended, and over at the piano the woman who did the playing was drawing up a chair and preparing to go to work.

"I'm not figuring on getting caught either," Mungor said finally, in his direct, quiet way. "I'm out to collect what I think's owed me — owed me for all the time I put in the army and that I lost because of the war. I've paid my dues in this damn life

21

twice over; now, it's only right I get a little of it back.

"And I will, too — know that for certain! I went clean through the war having men standing next to me die from bullets and bomb fragments and bayonets — and I never once got even a scratch. That told me something; I've got luck working for me — a charmed life, I reckon you could call it, and I ain't going to die except from old age.

"Meantime, I'm going to get everything I can by the only means I know how — and that's just taking it. I tried the other way, getting a job and such, but nobody'd even talk to me. They'd all forgot what I did for them in the army, that they owed me —"

"I don't figure nobody owes me nothing," Larch said, downing another drink. "Last time I got sent to the pen it was for something another jasper done. Was five years. Don't change nothing — was just the way the cards was dealt to me, and I'm ready to start all over. Only this time, like I said, ain't nobody going to ever lock me up again."

"Well, I'm for whatever needs doing to get me fifteen thousand dollars, or thereabouts," Sonny said. "You just call the shots, Mr. Mungor — when, where, and how — and we'll see how this here scheme of yours works."

"Reckon that settles it then," Mungor had said. He sensed a thread of doubt in the attitudes of both men but it didn't worry him; he could cure that in a hurry if all went well at the mine office in the Black Hills country.

"Plan on pulling out early in the morning," he had continued. "Meantime get your gear in shape and buy yourself some trail grub — stuff that won't need cooking — and stow it in your saddlebags. Time will come when we'll have to eat on the fly. Best you have a good canteen for water, too."

Larch, nodding, had said: "I'll be ready and waiting at the livery stable. Just you be there."

"You can count on it," Mungor replied dryly. "No need to tell the both of you to keep your mouth shut about what we're doing and where we're going. One word spilled to the wrong people" — Mungor shifted his eyes to bear directly on Sonny — "and everything could blow up in our faces."

The younger man drew up angrily. "Don't go fretting over me. I don't mix no business with pleasure. What I got to talk to them about ain't got nothing to do with working."

"I'll bank on that," Mungor had said.

"We be wearing masks and such?" Larch asked, refilling his glass again from the now near-empty bottle.

"Can use your neckerchief for a mask. I'll pick us up slickers to cover the rest — saw some gray ones in a store a few miles south of here. Best we pass up buying them here in Virginia City — could be a risk. . . . Anything else on your mind?"

Larch shook his head, glanced at Sonny. "Too late to back out now, boy, so if you've got something bothering you, best you get it straight now."

Sonny grinned. "Ain't nothing bothering me! I'm plain looking forward to being rich and having me a whole passel of women in my own place down in Mexico. I'm just rearing to get started at it!"

Mungor got to his feet. "See you in the morning then — early," he'd said and moved off in that ramrod-straight way of his.

3

They moved forward through the warm shadows at a quiet walk. Reaching the rear of the structure housing the mining company's office, Mungor raised a hand and silently signaled a halt. Drawing together, they dismounted, tied their horses to a nearby tree and, with spurs deadened by twigs wedged against the rowels, started along the side of the building.

Coming to the corner, Mungor again stopped and, still silent, drew his pistol and buttoned the long, gray slicker he was wearing. He waited until Sonny and Larch had completed a like procedure, and then throwing a final look at the mine to be certain no one was approaching, he nodded briskly to his partners, crossed swiftly to the door, and stepped inside.

"Nobody move!"

Mungor's hard voice was like a knife cutting through the heavy stillness that filled the cluttered room. The two men who had dropped by only minutes earlier were in a corner conversing with one of the office crew, apparently the head bookkeeper. All drew up sharply. The office employee blanched and then, glancing to the two remaining members of his force in the back of the room, shook his head.

Mungor moved quickly to the gate in the railing that separated the office proper from the remainder of the building, brushed it open, and entered.

"You're being smart. Stand quiet and nobody'll get hurt," he said and hurried to the closetlike cubicle in which the safe was kept.

Pausing, he looked over his shoulder. Things were going smoothly, like clockwork — just as he'd planned them. Sonny was at his assigned position inside the doorway, on watch for anyone coming from the mine or the road. Larch, pistol in each hand, was covering the three men in the corner and the pair sitting at a table in the rear where they had been poring over papers of some sort.

Satisfied, Mungor reached into the safe for the metal box sitting on one of the shelves. Logically, it would be the one in which the cash was kept. Opening it, a tight grin cracked his lips, breaking the usual severity of his features. The box was nearly filled with greenbacks and a number of double eagles and silver dollars. Closing the metal container, he tucked it under an arm and wheeled.

"Expect you know you won't get away with this," one of the men standing in the corner said in a promising voice.

"Nobody asked you nothing!" Larch snarled. "Just you keep your trap closed and you'll be alive to eat your vittles tonight!"

"Which sure'n hell's more'n you'll be doing!" the man replied. "By dark a posse'll have you all swinging from a —"

Larch had abruptly lunged forward. His right arm came around in a blurred arc. The pistol he was holding in his right hand struck the man alongside his head with a dull thud, dropped him to the dusty floor.

"Damn it — you've killed him!" one of the pair at the table shouted and came out of his chair.

Mungor, almost to the doorway, leveled his pistol at the man. "Settle down," he ordered quietly. "No need for getting yourself hurt, too."

He glanced at Sonny. The younger man nodded reassuringly. No one was coming. Again a smile parted the tall man's lips beneath his bandanna. Everything was still going as he'd planned — but more important, Larch had reacted to possible trouble in the manner that he'd hoped; he'd simply clubbed the man, who could have been a problem, and not shot him down.

"Want you all inside there with the safe," he ordered, wagging his pistol at the men. "Take your friend there on the floor with you. He ain't hurt bad."

The mining company employees at the table rose, began to edge toward the closet. Mungor eyed them closely. Neither was wearing a weapon. The two standing in the corner bent down, pulled the unconscious man to his feet. Only he was armed, and Larch, before Mungor could call attention to the fact, stepped forward and drew the weapon from its holster. Tossing it onto a nearby chair, the gunman resumed his position.

Once more Mungor looked to the doorway. Sonny responded with a nod. But time was beginning to run out, Mungor knew. They had been forced into a delay before making their move because of the couriers, and it was now drawing near quitting time for the men inside the mine. Instead of having ample time to leave the area, he and his partners would now have to make a fast departure and get well away from the mining company property before someone, reporting in at the office, discovered the men locked in the closet.

The last man was inside. Mungor closed the door quickly, turned the key in the lock, and dropped it into a cuspidor. Then, pivoting, he nodded to Larch and both retreated hurriedly to where Sonny was waiting.

"Nobody coming yet," the young man murmured. "This sure is going just like you said it would."

"Don't go crowing till we're out of here," Larch commented sourly as they stepped through the doorway into the lengthening shadows and doubled back along the building to where their horses were standing. "Which way we going?"

Swinging up onto his horse, Mungor pointed to the north, a course that would take them near the office. Larch, settling himself in his saddle, frowned disapprovingly.

"Just do what I tell you," Mungor said curtly.

They came about, raked their mounts with spurs and rushed past the office building, taking no pains to conceal the direction in which they were heading. Continuing for a good quarter mile, Mungor abruptly veered hard left, began to cut back through the pines on an almost due-south course. After a quarter hour or so he slowed the pace, allowed Larch and Sonny to draw up even with him.

"Sure had me guessing for a bit," the gunman said. "Recollected you saying we'd be working toward the south when we got done here."

Mungor shrugged. "Wanted them jaspers locked up in that office to hear us heading north so's they could tell the posse which way we went."

Sonny laughed. "They'll have themselves a nice little ride while we're going somewheres else!"

"It'll keep them busy for a spell," Mungor agreed and pointed to a line of bluffs a distance ahead. "We'll pull up there, blow the horses."

Larch again frowned his disapproval, possibly questioning the advisability of halting so soon, but he said nothing. Matters had gone just as Mungor had said they would and the gunman apparently wasn't about to challenge a good thing.

"This here'll do," Mungor said a short time later as he pulled up beneath a brushy overhang in the bluffs. It was almost full dark and he seemed in a hurry to accomplish something that he had in mind.

Dismounting, he dropped to his haunches and placing the metal cashbox taken from the mining company safe on the ground before him, opened it. Sonny, leaning over him with Larch at his side, whistled softly.

"Jeez! How much you reckon's there?"

Mungor made no reply, simply began to count the packs of currency — five hundred dollars in each — and then the gold and silver coins. Finished, he looked up.

"Four thousand and fifty dollars —"

Again Sonny whistled. "Four thousand — and it was easy — like shooting ducks in a pen!"

"That's the way all the jobs we'll be doing between here and Mexico will be — long as you listen to me," Mungor said, beginning to count out three piles of money. "I've got most of the places we'll be paying a visit to already planned out — just like that mine office. The rest I'll figure before we move in on them. Knowing what we're up against and how best to handle it, that's what makes it easy — and safe."

Hesitating, Mungor took up two of the stacks of greenbacks, each with five double eagles accompanying, and handed one to Larch, the other to Sonny.

"Here's five hundred dollars spending

money for you. Ought to last quite a spell if you handle it right."

"Five hundred dollars!" Sonny murmured in a breathless voice. "I ain't never seen that much money — not in my whole life!"

Larch had dropped the coins into a side pocket of his pants, was thumbing the currency slowly, lovingly. He said nothing, but Mungor could see in the gunman's dark features the reaction he was looking for: the sight of so much cash, easily and quickly obtained, had aroused the desire for more within him — just as it had in Sonny. He'd have no problem keeping them both in line now.

"Want to warn you about spending that," he said, thrusting his share into the small leather poke he carried. "Don't make a show of it. We don't want to draw anybody's attention — give them the idea that all of a sudden we've got a lot of money."

Rising, Mungor crossed to his horse, and unbuckling one of the saddlebags, obtained a canvas sack that he had provided. Opening it, he dumped the remainder of the money into it, tied the drawstrings tight, and held it up for his partners to see.

"Here's the start on the fifty thousand we're out to get. From now on we're on the move — fast and often."

"Suits me!" Sonny said joyfully, hurrying to his mount. "I'm rearing to go!"

Larch nodded, signifying his agreement as he went onto the saddle. Drawing his bottle of whiskey from the pocket of his slicker, he took a swallow, said, "What's next?"

"Cheyenne," Mungor replied, also mounting. "Bank there that's just right for cleaning out."

4

Hunched near the low fire, a cup of steam-ing black coffee in his hand, Sonny studied Mungor through hooded eyes. They had ridden well on to midnight before halting for the night and now, in the early light of the next morning, were preparing to move on to Cheyenne.

From his saddlebags, Mungor had pro-vided the coffee, the cups, and a blackened lard tin in which to make the brew. Evi-dently he carried no extra clothing, prefer-ring to use the space for items of food, minor gear, and the canvas bag in which they were to accumulate the money. He had said they would travel light and it was clear now to Sonny that he meant it. Before they rode on he reckoned he'd better take a look into his own saddlebags, see if there was anything he could do without, for he was convinced now that Mungor knew well what he was about and was worth patterning himself after.

The tall, hard-faced man had suddenly opened up a whole new world for him — a world in which his pockets were heavy with money and ripe with the promise of more to come. From that time on, Sonny vowed, nothing would be denied him; he could pick and choose his women — the high class, hoity-toity ones that were always beyond his reach and made it necessary that he settle for the hand-me-downs and the used-up ones. Not any more! Now he had the cash to buy himself the best!

And that went for everything else, too; fancy clothes, handmade boots, the best whiskey — although he wasn't much of a drinker — a right good saddle, and a fine horse. Hell, he'd fix himself up with everything that came to mind.

Dirt poor all of his life, he was sure going to make up for it now — or at least he would once they reached Mexico and it was safe to do some splurging.

Until then he'd play it close to the vest, do exactly as Mungor wanted him to do — even to the point of passing up a real inviting woman if it became necessary. Mungor was a bit hard to take at times, but he'd not question anything the man ordered him to do. Mungor had all the answers, and listening to him and following him was going to mean cash in his pocket — and that's what mattered.

According to Mungor, by the time they reached the Mexican border he would be rich beyond his wildest hopes, and if they kept on collecting greenbacks and double eagles at the rate they had begun — four thousand dollars in about fifteen minutes — it would be a lead-pipe cinch!

Larch stared into the fire absently. He was having problems figuring out Mungor. That the man had some schooling, that he had served in the army, and that he had once been a man of consequence was apparent. What, then, had brought him to the kind of life he was leading? What had turned him into an outlaw, one who, if things went the way he planned, would have every lawman west of the Missouri looking for him.

It had something to do with his time in the army — he'd said as much — and whatever it was, it had turned him inside out and made a hater out of him. But, hell, that was nothing special; what man didn't have something buried deep inside him, something that chawed at his innards continually and now and then came bubbling to the surface to make things miserable —

for himself and everybody around him?

Larch reckoned he'd probably never really know Mungor. He was not a man to talk about himself, and chances were better than good that he'd go to his grave without spilling whatever it was inside him to anybody — and that was jake with Ollie Larch. He had a few things jammed down in his own head that he'd as soon keep there — things that plain were nobody's business but his own. Likely that was exactly how Mungor felt.

But despite all, Mungor was a man to side. He knew what he was doing and where he was headed — and that was what counted. The man looked ahead, had a purpose for staying alive in a world where dying was easy, and Larch was figuring himself lucky to have had Mungor pick him as a partner.

The money would be welcome, of course, but that wasn't all there was to it; Mungor had provided him with a reason for living, had given him something to think about, to fill his mind with thoughts that sort of crowded out all the black shadows that plagued him. And, too, he now had a kind of a future to look forward to — if he was interested in one.

But it was the sort of life he liked and he'd

stick to Mungor as long as that was the way of it. He had a strong hunch, however, that Mungor wouldn't quit until he'd done what he had fixed in his mind — crossed the Mexican border with a fortune in his poke.

Fine . . . Larch was all for that, but if somewhere along the line things changed and Mungor started backing off from what he'd promised, that would be it and he'd pull off on his own. Long ago old Ollie Larch had learned it was smart to look out for number one.

Meantime, he'd make the most of it — hell, he'd be a damn fool not to grab on to the good luck that had suddenly come his way! But he'd not bank on it entirely; luck had a bad habit of running out on him right when everything was looking good, and it sure as hell could happen again. . . . Larch reached for his bottle, took a satisfying drink. . . . If things did go sour on him, he'd not be surprised and he'd be ready for it.

And the kid — Sonny. The same applied to him. He'd sort of taken the boy under his wing ever since that time in Missouri, and looked out for him, but after taking a hand in the robbery of the mining company and seeing Mungor in action — one of them smooth, cool-as-a-cucumber jaspers — the kid had lined up with Mungor one hundred per cent.

Good enough. He was glad that was how it would be; he'd be freer to make the most of his time. Larch paused in his thoughts, helped himself to another drink as a frown knotted his dark brow. On second thought, he reckoned he'd best keep on looking out for that woman-crazy kid. He was part of Mungor's plan — three men were necessary to carry it out Mungor had said — so, for his own sake, in protecting number one, he'd still better keep an eye on the boy.

But there was one thing that Mungor had best understand, and that was when and why he was to use his gun. He wasn't about to stand by and let some counterjumper take a free shot at him! He'd use his forty-five when and if he wanted — and if Mungor didn't like that, he knew damn well where he could go!

Mungor, collecting the empty cups and the lard tin in which he'd made coffee, returned them, along with the food that had been left over, to his saddlebags, and glanced to the horizon in the north once more; there was no sign of pursuit and he reckoned they had successfully thrown the posse off their trail.

Coming back around, he looked at Larch and Sonny. It hadn't been much of a breakfast, but he hadn't expected it to be and had long before told both of them that likely there would be many such times.

Neither had complained nor made mention of the fact, and that was good; he had them right where he wanted them now — right in the palm of his hand. The ease with which they had robbed the mining company office, and handing out five hundred dollars to each, had done the trick, just as he had been certain it would. Greed was always a powerful weapon of persuasion if a man knew how to use it — and he did.

The currency and gold double eagles were like an investment in the future for him. Giving it to them simply aroused their desire for more. Chances were neither of them had ever seen that much money at one time — much less had it for their own — and it undoubtedly had spoiled them, for neither would ever again be satisfied with just an ordinary job paying ordinary money; from now on they would think only of hundreds of dollars, of thousands, even, and dream also of the promised land below the Rio Grande.

Fine — but Mungor doubted if either would ever realize the dream. The law of averages would see to that; one, and most likely both, would die before they ever reached the border. He wasn't counting on it, of course, but the thought did lie in the back of his mind, along with the realization that if it worked out that way the entire amount they figured to accumulate, in the series of robberies they were embarking on, would be his.

His mind hesitated, thoughts darkening and becoming bitter as they switched to the woman who had been his wife. He wished Darsie — damn her black heart to hell — could know what lay in the future for him!

He'd have probably near fifty thousand dollars, all depending upon luck and the size of the prize they'd take from each of the dozen or so banks and stores that he'd lined up.

But again, averaging things out as he'd learned to do during the war, the sweep down from the Black Hills to the Mexican border should produce somewhere near that fifty-thousand figure — and with that he not only could live like a king, but he could be one!

There was no question in Dave Mungor's mind that such was his destiny. Sonny and Larch might make it, and perhaps they would get themselves killed. Not him! He was the one with the charmed life; the war had proven that.

5

They reached Cheyenne one afternoon shortly before dark. As they rode down the street Mungor called the attention of his partners to the bank. A narrow, one-story building sitting back off a corner, it had closed for the day.

"We'll take it in the morning — right after it opens," he said. "Won't be anybody around, hardly."

Sonny, looking ahead hungrily to the broad, ornate façade of the Silver Sage Saloon, nodded, said, "Sure — whenever you say."

Larch's thoughts, however, were not so far astray. "Why're we waiting for morning? Be better to bust in there tonight, blow the safe, and —"

"Can you handle gunpowder or dynamite?" Mungor cut in.

Larch shook his head. "No, ain't never done nothing like that. You being in the war and such, I figured you'd have the know-how."

"Wasn't in my duty. Not a good idea, anyway. Takes too long and the explosion wakes the whole town and can bring the law down on you fast. Odds are all against getting away in time."

Larch treated himself to a turn at his bottle of whiskey, brushed at his mouth with the back of a hand. "Expect you're right, but holding up a place in broad daylight's sort of risky, too, ain't it?"

"Not much. I'd rather do it late in the day, just before they close. Streets are empty then — most folks being at home eating supper — but early morning's not so bad. Hardly anybody stirring then, too, and it's easy to just walk in quietlike, help ourselves, and leave. Can be well on the way to Denver before the alarm goes up."

"That where we're going next — Denver?" Larch wondered aloud.

"Number three on my list," Mungor replied. "Only a hundred miles or so from here, and the bank I've got spotted'll be a cinch."

"We putting up at the Silver Sage?" Sonny, a bit out ahead of Mungor and Larch, called back. "Looks like a mighty fancy place."

"The best in town," the tall man answered.

"Pull around behind it — stable's there. Want to get these horses looked after. Been a long day for them."

Sonny turned to Larch. "You mind seeing to this broomtail of mine? I'm sort of in a hurry to get inside and —"

"Nope — got my own horse to look after," Larch said bluntly.

Mungor shook his head as the younger man shifted his attention to him. "Better take the time. Something could go wrong tomorrow and we might have to make a run for it — and if your animal gives out, it'll mean you're through because Larch and me won't be stopping to help."

The gunman muttered his sanction, again treated himself to a drink. There were only a few people on the street, now coming alive with lamplight from the windows of the stores along the way, and none appeared to notice the three riders moving slowly by.

"Could do it later," Sonny said, placing it in the form of a suggestion.

"Yeh, reckon you could. It's up to you, but you best get this straight in your head: that horse is a hell of a lot more important than any woman —"

"I know that," Sonny broke in impatiently as they pulled up in front of the stable. "Don't need to keep ragging me about it."

Mungor sat quietly in his saddle for a long breath, his moody, gray eyes fixed on the younger man. "I don't aim to," he said finally. "Not again — ever."

A quick smile spread across Sonny's face. "I ain't meaning that the way it sounded," he said, apologetically. "Just that it's been a spell since —"

His words halted as Mungor, paying no attention, swung down and, gathering in the reins of his horse, led it into the stable. An elderly man appeared at once, nodding first to Mungor and then to Larch and Sonny.

"Yes, sir, gents. What all will you be needing?"

"Everything," Sonny said hurriedly. "Want my horse rubbed and grained and looked after real good — and I'm ready to pay right generous for doing it. Somebody around I can depend on doing it —"

"Me," the hostler said. "Be a dollar for rubbing him down, another'n for the oats and hay, and then fifty cents for the night."

"I ain't interested in what it'll cost — only that it'll get done," Sonny said, digging into a pocket for the necessary coins. Thrusting the reins and the silver into the man's hands, he wheeled, started for the door. "Aim to drop by later on, see that he's been looked after."

The hostler stared after him for a moment or two, then brought his attention back to Mungor and Larch.

"He's sure in a powerful hurry. It whiskey or women?"

"Women," Larch said dryly.

"Well, there's a plenty of them in there, just waiting for the likes of him. Some mighty-fine lookers, too. Now, you be wanting your horses took care of the same as his'n?"

"Same," Mungor said, "only I'll do the rubbing down of mine. Need to look him over close. Been using him hard."

"Then take him into the back stall — and you, mister, can use the one next him if you're doing the same. . . . Where'd you all come from?"

"Up Wichita way," Mungor said blandly.

"Far piece, all right," the stableman said and moved off down the runway with Sonny's bay.

For the ensuing three-quarters of an hour Mungor and Larch worked with their mounts, rubbing them down with coarse feed sacks, examining their hoofs for splits and objects wedged in the frogs, making certain the shoes were tight and not likely to come loose. That done, and seeing to it that both animals were watered and had an

46

ample supply of grain and fresh hay, they hung their saddlebags over their shoulders and, crossing the dark, open yard to the saloon, climbed the half a dozen steps to the back door and entered.

Although it was still early evening, there was considerable activity in the place — a wide, almost square room — the walls of which were decorated with numerous distillery calendars and prize-fight posters — filled with tables and chairs. A bar ran across one side, a second-floor balcony the other, while gambling equipment and a piano, with a small cleared area for dancing, occupied the two remaining.

Stepping up to the bar Mungor and Larch each ordered whiskey. When it came, Mungor paid for both and, pivoting, hooked his elbows on the rolled edge of the counter and let his glance travel the fairly crowded, smoky room in search of Sonny.

There was no sign of him. Mungor raised his eyes to the balcony. The girls would have their rooms up there; no doubt that was where Sonny would be found. He heard Larch call for a second drink, tossed off his and, turning back, slid his glass toward the bartender with a nod.

"Place around here where a man can get a meal?" he asked.

The aproned man nodded, jerked a thumb toward a door in the rear of the saloon. "In there. Woman runs a restaurant."

Mungor said, "Obliged. How about a room for the night?"

The bartender pushed the shot glass of whiskey to him. "Sure — upstairs; but ain't you with that young cowhand — one that calls himself Sonny — that just come in?"

Mungor nodded.

"Well, he's expecting you — room Five. Says he's got a right nice surprise waiting for you two fellows."

Mungor glanced at Larch. "Can guess what kind of a surprise he's rigged up — women."

The gunman downed his drink, called for another. "Can bet on it. . . . You got something against women?"

Mungor shrugged. "Nothing, just don't have much time for them any more. Once had one — wife, in fact. I thought she was the most beautiful thing alive — and I reckon she was."

Larch studied the liquor in his glass. "What happened to her? She dead?"

Again Mungor's wide shoulders stirred. "No, she ran off with another man while I was away fighting the war — but if I ever come across her, she will be. I aim to kill

48

her. She ruined my life."

Larch considered the tall man's hard, set features for a long moment and then, finishing off his drink, dropped a coin on the counter in payment and turned away.

"Let's go see what that fool kid's got fixed up for us. I figure we both could stand a mite of hell raising."

Silent, Mungor wheeled and, with Larch at his side, crossed to the narrow stairway and climbed to the upper floor. He hesitated there, eyes probing along the dimly lit hallway for the proper room. Number Five was about halfway down the left side. Moving on, the two reached the designated room, halted. They could hear the clink of glasses, muted conversation, and an occasional burst of laughter coming from within. Raising a hand, Mungor rapped on the door and, grasping the knob, pushed it open.

A shout from Sonny and the overpowering smell of perfume and lilac water greeted them. The younger man was sitting on the edge of the bed, a drink in one hand, an arm around a dark-haired pretty girl wearing a yellow dress. Seated on chairs nearby were two more women, both young and equally pretty.

"What the hell took you jaybirds so long?"

Sonny demanded, laughing. "We been setting here waiting and waiting!"

"Didn't know you would be —" Mungor began.

"Figured that I'd surprise you! Now, I've done bought out three rooms — this'n and the ones next to it. The ladies go with them. Way I see it we've got us a stem-winder of a whing-ding coming!"

Mungor's eyes narrowed. Larch swore deeply. Sonny lifted his glass high, swung it about in a circle, spilling some of its contents.

"After all that hard work we been doing over in Kansas — punching them damned cows, trail driving, and such — we've sure earned us a celebration!"

The lines in Mungor's square face softened and a thread of relief entered his eyes. Sonny was being careful after all; he guessed he'd sold the younger man a bit short.

"Sounds like a good idea," he said with a side glance at Larch.

The gunman was staring fixedly at one of the women, a blonde with a black beauty mark on one cheek and wearing a short dress that exposed her well-shaped legs.

"It sure is," Larch said in a thick voice and, stepping up to the yellow-haired girl, grasped her by the hand and pulled her to her feet. "Come on, girlie — let's get going."

The blonde laughed and, hurrying to keep up with Larch as he moved toward the door, waved back at her two friends. "I reckon I've been spoke for!" she said as they disappeared into the hallway.

Mungor turned his attention to the remaining woman, casting a quick glance at Sonny, already busy with his choice.

"Looks like it's you and me," he said to her. "Name's Dave."

The girl — dark-haired, blue-eyed, and slender — smiled. "Guess so. I'm Florinda. What do you want to do first?"

Mungor rubbed at the stubble on his jaw. "Clean up a mite, then get something to eat. The night's young."

"Sure is. We can go to my room, start there. I've got a tub — can heat some water."

Mungor's usually stolid expression broke. He smiled. "Lead the way. I'm all yours."

6

"We wearing them slickers?" Larch asked when they drew to a stop at the end of the passageway separating the Cheyenne bank from its neighboring structure.

Mungor shook his head. "Could draw attention. This time use only your mask. Pull it up over your face when we step inside." He hesitated, glanced at Sonny. The younger man had been awake most of the night, he suspected, and he was having doubts about him.

"You for sure you're ready?"

Sonny grinned, stifled a yawn. "You bet! Just lead off — I'll be right there with bells on. Having a woman always fixes me up fine as frog hair."

Mungor nodded, waited while Larch secured the horses to a post at the end of the passage, evidently the remains of what had once been a fence, and then, moving to the corner of the bank building, threw his glance along the street. There was no one near, but he could see several pedestrians farther along the way.

"The place open yet?" Larch asked, shifting his holstered gun forward.

"It's open," Mungor replied. "Now, we walk together, going and coming. No running — no matter what comes up. Keep your mask on while we're in the bank, slip it off when we're outside — unless we run into trouble —"

"We won't," Sonny declared confidently. "Ain't nobody around to give us any."

Mungor felt the side pocket of his brush jacket, made certain the pieces of cord he'd provided were there, and then, with Sonny and Larch at either shoulder, stepped out of the passageway and walked casually toward the entrance to the bank. Down the street where the fields began, birds were singing cheerfully and from somewhere close by a dog had begun to bark.

"Be two men in there — leastwise that's how it was when I looked the place over," Mungor said. "The teller and the owner."

"Kind of a little outfit," Larch muttered. "Ain't likely to get much cash."

"Maybe not, but taking on the big places means a lot more risk. Always more hired help around — six or eight at least. And

53

customers are more plentiful."

"Yeh, reckon so," the gunman said, his gaze reaching to the far end of the street where a man in a buckboard was coming toward them.

Mungor had seen it too. He slowed the pace to where they would not reach the bank's doorway too soon. The buckboard driver came on, dozing apparently on the seat. He gained the intersection — turned off. Larch swore softly in relief.

"Would've been all right if he'd passed by," Mungor said. "We're just three men looking for a restaurant so's we can get a bite to eat. No call to fret."

They had come to the door of the bank, standing open in the interest of keeping the place cool for the day. Mungor turned in at once, Larch and Sonny following. The latter halted just inside, took up his usual position where he could keep watch on the street.

Mask in place, Mungor glanced hurriedly about. There were two men on the job, as he had previously noted; one stood behind the wire, fronting the teller's cage, the other was seated at a desk. Both drew up slowly, arms raising as they beheld Larch and Mungor with leveled pistols.

"Just keep quiet and you'll not get hurt," Mungor said and, brushing past the man at

54

the desk, crossed to the safe standing against the wall. Reaching it, he beckoned to the teller.

"Get over there with your boss," he ordered, and as the man hurried to comply, he began to gather in the packets of currency neatly stacked on one of the shelves in the thick-walled iron box. There were no sacks handy and he was forced to stuff the currency inside his shirt.

That done, he glanced about. There should be a supply of gold coins somewhere. Mungor located them in the teller's cage and, entering swiftly, scooped them into a pocket of his jacket, all the while ignoring the silver.

The sudden, muffled crack of a small-caliber pistol brought him about. He saw Larch rock to one side while nearby the owner of the bank, a derringer in his hand, was frantically trying to open a drawer in his desk where he evidently kept a larger pistol.

Mungor swore, lunged across the room. Larch was a step before him, arm raised, poised. It came down fast, the weapon in his hand thudding against the banker's head, knocking him senseless to the floor.

Mungor, pressed by a feeling of urgency, hurriedly pulled the cord from his pocket and glanced toward Sonny. The lone gun-shot, while from a small pistol, might have been heard nevertheless.

"Ain't nobody in sight," the younger man said.

At once Mungor jerked the teller about, tied his wrists behind him, and then, using the bandanna he found in the man's pocket, gagged him tightly. Pushing him aside, he wheeled to the banker.

Larch, blood staining the left sleeve of his shirt, had rolled the man over, was tying his hands together. Squatting beside him, Mun-gor muffled the banker with a handkerchief and, rising, looked closely at the gunman.

"You hit bad?"

"Bleeding some, but it ain't much more'n a scratch. We all done here?"

Mungor said, "Just about," and pointed to a partition across the back of the room that created an area apparently used for storage purposes. "Let's put these two in there and shut the door. That'll keep them from draw-ing somebody's attention for a spell."

Shoving the teller ahead of him, Mungor took the banker by one foot, Larch seized the other, and together they dragged the unconscious man into the adjoining room. Leaving him on the floor, with the teller, eyes filled with fright, standing nearby, they closed the door, and moments later were again on the sidewalk, sauntering toward the passageway where their horses waited. Within a quarter hour they were well out of town, riding northward. Abandoning that small measure of precaution after a mile or two, they began to circle and soon were on the road to Denver.

Side by side, their horses at an easy lope, Mungor cast a critical eye at Larch. The gunman was staring straight ahead, jaw set, eyes partly closed. Mungor could see that each jarring step of his mount sent pain surging through the man.

"Be stopping soon's we're well clear," he said. "Want to take that bottle of whiskey you've got in your saddlebags and pour a little on that bullet wound. No chance of us getting to a doctor until we reach Denver."

"That damned little fool!" Larch said feelingly and spat into the loose dust of the road. "Sure never figured him for trying to be a hero. . . . How much cash you reckon we got?"

"Never took time to look it over," Mungor replied. "I'll do some counting when we stop to blow the horses and fix your arm."

Larch shook his head. "Hell, I'll be all right. Been hurt worse falling off a saddle."

"No doubt, but if we don't disinfect the

place with something, you could get blood poisoning — and that's sure what you don't want."

Larch stirred indifferently, jerked his head at a grove of trees off to their right. "Expect that'd be a good place. Looks like there might be water."

Mungor signified his agreement, and together the three men swung off the road and crossed to the cluster of trees. There was a spring that created a small, clear pool and they halted beside it.

They dismounted and Sonny, who had been dozing, led the horses off a short distance while Mungor set to work immediately on the wound in Larch's arm — soaking it first in the pool in order to remove the part of the sleeve that had dried with blood and was sticking to the ragged opening in the arm.

That accomplished, Mungor washed the wound thoroughly and then, with the gunman cursing vividly, poured a quantity of the whiskey from the bottle Sonny had brought from the man's saddlebags onto the raw flesh.

Stepping back, he handed the bottle to Larch, said: "Expect you need a little of this on the inside, now. Take a couple of swallows and we'll pull out. Sooner we get to a doctor, the better for you."

Larch mumbled something, tipped the bottle to his lips and took several long swallows. Sonny, sprawled alongside the spring, pulled himself to an elbow, centered his attention on Mungor.

"You going to count that money?"

Mungor said, "Yeh, reckon so, but we best take a minute to think about this — we got a bit careless back there. Ended up with one of us getting shot. If that'd been a six-shooter, we could all be dead right now. Next time we best see to it that there's no weapons handy."

"Amen," Sonny murmured.

Larch only shrugged, watched as Mungor began to remove the packs of currency from inside his shirt and place them on the grassy ground. Counting the bills, he then produced the gold coins, added them to the pile.

"A little more'n three thousand," he said and, as Sonny whistled his appreciation, gathered the money up, moved to his horse, and dumped it into the canvas sack that was in a saddlebag. "Brings the total up to around five thousand five hundred — not counting what's in our pockets."

A half-smile parted Larch's lips. "Now, that sure ain't bad for a couple or three country boys! I'm sure liking this way of making a living."

"Me too," Sonny declared. "We're getting rich fast. We still going to clean us out one of them Denver banks after Larch gets his arm fixed up?"

"Just what I'm planning," Mungor said, "and the one I've lined up ought to be worth plenty — but first we've got to get Larch to a doctor. A one-armed man won't be any good to us. . . . Let's pull out."

7

It was shortly after noon when Mungor and his partners reached the outskirts of Colorado's largest city. Larch, now in considerable pain, maintained a tight-lipped silence as they entered a tree-lined street, but Sonny, having caught up on his sleep during the previous night and following day, was in high, good spirits and looking forward to the next robbery.

"You figure we'll take as much from this bank here as we got at that one in Cheyenne?" he asked.

Mungor, eyes on a woman tending a small garden plot a short distance east of the road, nodded, said: "Ought to come through with more. . . . Keep riding, you two. I'll see if I can find out about a doctor from that lady over here."

He swung away at once, rode to the edge of the yard where the woman was hoeing. Dismounting, Mungor removed his hat and walked a few steps nearer.

"Ma'am, one of my friends had an accident," he said indicating Larch and Sonny. "There a doctor around here close?"

The woman leaned on her hoe, brushed at the hair in her eyes, and considered him briefly. "Yep, reckon there is," she said, finally, pointing on down the street. "Be about a half mile. Name's Gilmore."

"I'm obliged to you," Mungor said, replacing his hat and turning away.

"What kind of a accident?" the woman called after him.

Mungor gave that quick thought. He might as well make no mention of a gunshot wound. "He fell off his saddle," he said and, climbing back onto his horse, spurred to overtake his partners.

"Doctor's on ahead a piece," he reported. "Name's Gilmore. Watch for his sign."

They spotted the physician's combination office and residence shortly thereafter and pulled in alongside. Coming off his mount, Mungor hung his saddlebags over a shoulder and turned to Sonny.

"Take the horses around back out of sight. Strangers sometimes make lawmen curious. Take a look-see if there's anybody else on the place, too. I'll go on in with Larch; you come in when you're finished."

He didn't wait to hear a response from Sonny but, walking a stride in front of Larch, stepped up to the door of the office, on which was the invitation COME IN, and entered.

The waiting room was small, furnished with half a dozen chairs and a table. There was no one visible but at the tinkling of a bell affixed to the top of the door and tripped by its opening, a young and pretty girl wearing a white apron over a gingham dress appeared.

"Yes?" she said, smiling. "Can I do something for you?"

Hat in hand again, Mungor said: "We want to see the doctor, miss. My friend here's been hurt."

A slight frown replaced the smile on the girl's face. She hesitated, started to turn and re-enter the room from which she had come. At that moment a florid-faced, middle-aged man in a gray suit appeared in the doorway.

"Who is it, Jenny?"

"Some men to see you, Papa. One's been hurt, but I —"

The physician, distinguished in his spade beard and neatly trimmed mustache, silenced the girl with a wave of his hand. He eyed Larch sharply, shook his head.

"Gunshot wound — but I don't treat out-laws."

Mungor's cold smile reflected no humor. "What makes you think we're outlaws?"

"Doesn't take much sense to figure that out," Gilmore said.

"Well, it's neither here nor there," Mungor said, drawing his pistol; "you're treating him. Now, get busy at it, Doc. I'd hate to cause you trouble."

Gilmore began to back up, leading Larch into what was his treatment room. The door opened in the next moment and Sonny entered, paused, glanced about.

"Ain't nobody else around," he said, his eyes halting on Jenny Gilmore. "Howdy, lady. I sure ain't never seen no nurse pretty as you!"

Jenny smiled in spite of herself and turned away.

Gilmore, motioning Larch into a chair beside a metal edged table, nodded to the girl. "I'll need hot water — and then I want you to run over to the Quints's and —"

"She's not going anywhere — not for a while," Mungor cut in quietly and motioned to Sonny. "Stay with her. Don't let her out of your sight."

"Sure thing," Sonny replied happily and took the girl by the arm. "Come on, honey, let's you and me go get that water your pa's wanting."

For a moment Jenny appeared to resist and then, as if unable to withstand the charm of his smile, she pivoted and led the way into the adjoining room.

Thoughtful, Mungor put his attention on the physician, now examining Larch's wound with a deep frown puckering his brow.

"Asking you again, Doc — what makes you think we're outlaws?"

Gilmore did not look up. "You fit the description the sheriff got from Cheyenne of three men that robbed the bank there a couple of days ago. Said one wore an old army hat. Another one was young, little more than a boy. And one got himself shot in the arm."

Mungor brushed at the sweat on his face. It was hot in the small room. He hadn't expected the word to travel so fast — and if the lawmen in Denver had been warned, so would all others in the area.

The inner door opened and the girl, with Sonny carrying a kettle of steaming water, entered. She showed him where to set it, and then opening a glass-fronted case in which there were several bottles of medicine and rolls of bandages, stepped back.

Gilmore at once made a pad of gauze and began to clean the wound in Larch's arm, muttering something about it having been scalded.

"Had to disinfect with something," Mungor explained, absently. "Used whiskey."

The physician made no comment, continued to work. Nearby, Sonny, his attention on Jenny, said, "Ain't hardly room for all of as in here. Why don't you and me go set in the kitchen, talk?"

The girl hesitated, glanced at her parent who seemed too engrossed to hear. Abruptly she turned and, with Sonny following closely, retreated into the adjoining room, closing the door behind them.

Larch raised his eyes to Mungor, winked slyly. No doubt Sonny would keep Jenny Gilmore occupied for as long as it was necessary.

But Mungor was not thinking about Sonny and what he might be doing; he had more serious things on his mind. The word was out and the law would be on the watch for them. First of all they would need to change their appearance — which wouldn't be hard to do — and make use again of the slickers he had earlier provided. It probably had been a mistake to not wear them at Cheyenne, but he had feared they would attract attention, do more harm than good. He reckoned he'd been wrong; hereafter they'd make use of them, regardless — but they'd best also change their clothing — hats particularly.

He heard Larch swear deeply and, from the corner of an eye, saw him flinch. Gilmore had poured some sort of antiseptic into the wound, and was now preparing to apply a salve of some sort, and bind it.

Mungor crossed to a window and glanced out. They weren't too far from the center of the town, and it would be foolish not to go ahead with plans to rob the bank. Such would simply be a matter of waiting out the remainder of the afternoon until the proper time to make a move was at hand, and then proceed.

"Going to be a little stiff," he heard Gilmore say, "but it'll be all right in a few days."

Larch, evidently much relieved, broke the tight silence that had gripped him. "Sure mighty glad to hear that. How much I owe you?"

Gilmore, washing his hands, shook his head. "Nothing — and I don't want it said that I treated you."

Larch tossed two silver dollars onto the table. "You're getting paid anyway, Doc," he said harshly. "I ain't taking no favors from nobody like you!"

Again the physician wagged his head. "I won't take it — and I want you out of my house — right now!"

"Can't do that, Doc," Mungor said. "We're going to be your guests for a couple of hours more, so you might as well lock your front door and settle down. We'll be leaving about dark."

8

"Let's go," Mungor said quietly and, stepping out of the alleyway, he started up the walk for the door of the bank. Sonny and Larch, wearing their long, gray slickers, as was he, were at his side.

They had delayed until almost five o'clock when the bank would close — a fact ascertained by Mungor at the time he had the place under observation. They had no fear of an alarm being raised by Gilmore or his daughter, Jenny; both had been left securely tied and gagged in one of the rooms at the physician's residence.

There was no way of knowing if there were customers inside the building; it was a chance they had to take, but Mungor's earlier observation had also revealed that patrons were rare at that late hour of the day, just as there would be few persons on the street.

In a tight knot, masks pulled up over their

faces, they stepped through the doorway into the shadowy depths of the building and halted. There was a customer at one of the two tellers' windows transacting business of some sort. Elsewhere in the room were two men seated at roll-top desks while a woman worked over a sheaf of papers on a long table just beyond them.

It was unnecessary for Mungor to speak the words customary at such moments; their drawn pistols, masks, and all-concealing slickers were sufficient. The bank employees, and their solitary patron, all raised their hands quickly.

"Close that door," Mungor said to Sonny, and then crossing to the usual railing that separated the employee area from the lobby, stepped over it and started toward the open safe in the back of the room. "Keep an eye on them this time," he added pointedly to Larch.

The thick-shouldered gunman stirred, muttered something unintelligible under his mask, and moved in closer to where he had a better view of all concerned.

"Don't try nothing," he said then in a muffled, warning tone. "As soon shoot you as spit."

Mungor heard the words, paused in his gathering of currency from the shelves in the safe, and glanced over a shoulder to see what had evoked the cautioning. No one had stirred. He guessed Larch was just making certain that none of those present got any ideas. That the gunman was a bit jumpy after his previous experience with the bank owner in Cheyenne was evident — and understandable.

The haul was going to be a good one, Mungor realized with satisfaction as he put the last of the paper money in a canvas sack he found in the safe. There would be several thousand, at least. Wheeling, he threw a hasty look at Sonny for reassurance. The younger man nodded, as was the preagreed signal, that all was clear. Mungor hurried on to the first of the tellers' cages.

He collected a considerable amount of currency and a few gold eagles in one, didn't fare as profitably in the second as the teller, evidently in the act of closing for the day, had already removed most of his cash to the safe.

Tightening the drawstring of the bag, Mungor thrust it inside his slicker and under his shirt, intentionally left unbuttoned and, again drawing his pistol, rejoined Larch. As was the way back in the mining company office, the safe stood within a specially built closet. This one, Mungor noted, had an especially thick door and a heavy lock designed, apparently, with the thought of making the money doubly safe.

"Inside — all of you," he ordered, motioning with his pistol.

Everyone, with the exception of the customer, started toward the small room. He came around suddenly. A wild look filled his eyes.

"I ain't getting in there!" he shouted and ran for the door.

Sonny's gun came up. The blast filled the room with thundering echoes. The man pitched forward, went full length on the floor, and lay still.

Mungor swore deeply, glared at Sonny through the drifting layers of powder smoke. Crossing quickly to the prone figure, he knelt beside it.

"Dead," he muttered after a moment and rising put his attention again on the younger man. "What the hell's the matter with you?" Without waiting for any reply, he pivoted to Larch. "We best get out of here fast. That gunshot probably was heard."

Larch was already herding the bank employees into the safe closet. Mungor stepped up to its door, and as the last member entered, he closed the thick panel and turned the key.

"Anybody coming?" he called to Sonny.

The younger man swept the street in both directions with his eyes. "Nope — nobody."

Mungor smiled grimly, said, "We're lucky — so far," and beckoned to Larch. "Got to drag the dead man back out of sight so's somebody looking in won't see him and holler for the law. I've got a hunch we need to be a far piece from here when they find out about this."

Wordless, Larch moved to his side. Together they moved the unfortunate bank customer's body in behind the desks, and then returned quickly to the door where Sonny was standing watch.

"Still ain't seen nobody coming."

Mungor said, "Good! We're going to need a head start after that fool stunt you pulled."

"Fool stunt — hell!" Sonny shot back angrily. "You figure I ought to've just stood there, let him gun me down?"

Mungor jerked open the door, surveyed the street. He could see several persons a hundred yards or so down the way, one of whom was looking in the direction of the bank. There was no one near, however.

"He wasn't armed," Mungor said, continuing to eye the man facing toward them, and then, as the man turned away, added: "Let's get away from here," and pulling down his mask, stepped out onto the sidewalk.

Sonny, hard on his heels, swore angrily. "How was I going to know that? He was coming straight at me, aiming to run for it. I fired 'cause I figured he'd have a gun."

"Should've made sure," Mungor said, closing the door and moving off down the walk toward the alleyway where they had left the horses.

"That's damn fool talking," Larch observed dryly. "I'd a done the same, was I the kid. Man ain't got time be wondering at a time like that. Get off the kid's back, Mungor."

They had reached the alley, turned in. Mungor, without slowing, gave Larch a hard, direct look. "If you don't like the way I'm running this, pull out. I'll hand over your share, give you what you've got coming."

The gunman, jerking the lines of his horse free of the post to which he'd secured them, thrust a foot into a stirrup. Hesitating, he grinned at Mungor.

"Hell with that! I know a good thing when I see it — and you and me are staying partners till we get to the border. Where we heading now?"

Mungor, his temper aroused by what he

felt was interference on Larch's part, settled himself in his saddle and swung his horse about. He had been somewhat surprised by Sonny's actions, believing that if there were any killings it would be Larch who committed them.

"North," he said, coming back to the gunman's question.

"North? What're we going that way for? Ain't nothing but little jerkwater burgs —"

"I know that," Mungor cut in as they reached the end of the alley and turned into the road leading from the settlement. "We've got to get rid of these duds we're wearing. Description's out on us."

"Can stop at the next town."

"No, would be giving ourselves away — all of us walking in buying new clothes. Be smarter to find us a homesteader or a rancher, get some from him — old stuff that's been worn. Once we do that we can head east for Buffalo City."

9

Deputy Sheriff Ben Houston was a squat, stubborn man with waning hopes. In his late thirties, he had been a secondary lawman all of his adult life, had continually entertained ambitions to succeed Sheriff Ed Bryan when he resigned. Now that said day was at hand, he was beginning to worry; he had no firm assurance from the county powers that he would be taking the ailing Bryan's place.

Politics being what they were, it just could be that a certain outsider who had good connections would be pinning on the lawman's star which he would wear until the forthcoming election when, as the candidate of the party in control, his position would be made permanent by the voters.

"It's going to be up to you," Bryan said, rubbing nervously at the back of his neck. "I ain't able to go — and I sure can't send Hooker. He ain't good for nothing but

76

sweeping out and tending the jail."

Houston, leaning against the wall of the sheriff's office, arms folded over his chest, nodded slowly.

"Anyways," Bryan continued, "you're the only man I figure can track them killers down. You've got the savvy — and you've got the experience. Hell of a thing, them riding in here, bold as brass, robbing one of our banks and killing a citizen — and then riding off big as you please!"

"They're smart," Houston said. "No doubt of that."

"Maybe so, but I ain't yet seen the outlaw that was smart enough to beat the law every time. Sooner or later something's going to trip him up."

Houston nodded. He'd been in the office poring over wanted dodgers that previous night, when Stanley Mott had come rushing in to report the bank holdup and the murder of Dallas McGee, a homesteader from south of town.

Mott had scarcely left after giving what description he could — three men, masked and wearing long, gray slickers — when Doc Gilmore showed up to tell how three men, one of them slightly wounded, had arrived at his home, forced him to treat the injured man, and then held him and his daughter prisoners in a back room until dark.

The men answered the description of those who had held up the bank in Cheyenne, he'd pointed out, and he was certain they were one and the same. They seemed to be planning something there in Denver, but he wasn't sure just what it was since they never did come right out and talk about it.

"Well, they robbed Charlie Pollard's bank," Sheriff Bryan had said, "and killed Dallas McGee while they was doing it."

"McGee!" the physician had echoed, shocked. "Why, he was in to see me this morning. Was having trouble with his foot. Why in the world would they want to kill him?"

"Stan Mott said that Dallas sort of lost his head. Was in there making a payment on his mortgage when that bunch walked in. He tried to rush the outlaw standing guard at the door — got shot down doing it. They harm you any?"

Gilmore shrugged. "No, they were decent enough to me and Jenny, I suppose, for their kind."

"She there at the time?" Houston wanted to know.

"Yes. I tried to send her out on an excuse so's she could get word to one of you. Was no doubt in my mind who they were — but I didn't get away with it. Head man, a big, tall fellow wearing an old U.S. Army hat, stopped her and told the young one to keep an eye on her."

Bryan leaned forward in his chair, elbows on his littered desk. His ruddy face was intent; his small, black eyes were narrowed.

"You get a good look at them? Or was they wearing masks and slickers?"

"No — had on regular clothes, like ordinary cowhands wear."

Bryan settled back. He glanced at Houston and nodded in satisfaction. "Seems we're getting lucky, Deputy. We've got somebody who can give us a description of that bunch."

Houston smiled briefly, turned to Gilmore. "I can use all the help you can give me when it comes to identifying them, Doc. I'm starting out on a cold trail and every little bit's going to come in handy."

Gilmore stroked his beard thoughtfully for a moment or two and then began a description of each outlaw. When he had finished, he said: "Could be I've left out something, so it might be smart to drop by the place and talk to Jenny. She can tell you more about the young one than I can."

"I'll do that, Doc," Houston had said as

the physician turned to leave. "Didn't any of them ever call one of the others by name?"

Gilmore gave that thought, shook his head. "Was careful about that," he'd replied. "None of them ever did."

Now, the following morning, preparatory to pulling out, Houston was going over final details with Bryan.

"Maybe I don't have any names," he said, "but I've got pretty fair descriptions. Picking out the bird that seems to be running the outfit won't be hard, and there won't be no trouble spotting the other two — a heavy-set fellow with a bandage on one arm and a kid that smells like he just came out of a barbershop —"

"You keep remembering he's the one that cut down Dallas McGee, so don't let him being young and having curly hair and a friendly smile fool you. He's a cold-blooded killer."

"Ain't likely to forget," Houston said, getting to his feet. "Reckon I'd best pull out. Got my horses ready and sooner I start asking questions around, sooner I'll get on their trail."

"You turn up anybody that seen them leaving town so's you'll know which way they went?"

"Nope, not yet, but expect I will —"

Houston paused. A frown knotted his face as he glanced out the window to the street where a light farm wagon had pulled up in front of the office. The driver was Callie Yarbro. Huddled on the seat beside her was her teen-age daughter, Melly, and in the bed of the vehicle lay a blanket-covered figure.

"Who is it?" Bryan asked, not rising.

"The Yarbros," the deputy answered. "Looks like something bad's happened."

Pivoting, the deputy crossed to the door and hurried out into the warm sunlight, hearing Bryan hastily get to his feet and follow. Together they stepped up to the wagon and looked more closely at the haggard features of the woman.

"What's the trouble, Mrs. Yarbro?" Bryan said, laying his hand on her arm.

The woman appeared not to hear at first, and then stirring wearily, she pointed at the figure under the blanket.

"That's my mister — Joe. They killed him —"

Houston turned to the wagon bed, lifted the cover. "It's him all right. Been shot through the head."

Bryan, his features stiff, put his attention back on the woman. "What happened, Callie? Who killed him?"

"Didn't only kill him," she said woodenly. "One of them took my girl, Melly, into the barn and used her. Another'n caught me and —"

"Rape," Bryan muttered. "Who were they, Callie? You know them?"

The woman shook her head. "Was three of them. One had a bandage on his arm. Been hurt, I reckon. He was the one that caught me. Another'n was young — not much more'n a boy. Was him that ruined Melly."

"The same bunch," Bryan muttered in a low, savage voice. "Another killing — and now they've abused a woman and a girl."

Houston had stepped back. Motioning to a man standing on the opposite side of the street and a short distance away looking at them wonderingly, he called: "Go get Doc Gilmore, Jesse."

Bryan was holding the woman's hand as if trying to comfort her. "Why'd they kill Joe?"

Callie Yarbro fixed her lifeless gaze on him, shrugged. "No reason, 'cepting he tried to stop them. They come to the house a time after dark. Was looking for a place to stay the night. Said they'd pay. The mister told them they could bunk in the barn and that if they was hungry we'd feed them."

The woman's voice, slow and heavy with

grief and exhaustion, broke. The girl beside her was sobbing quietly, face hidden by the shawl she had drawn over her head.

"They went to the barn like they was told," Callie continued, "then come up to the house. The mister let them in and they had some supper. Was only leftovers. We'd done et.

"When they was through, the tall one — expect he was in the army once because he was wearing some of a uniform — got up and said they was needing clothes. He didn't ask if he could buy them or anything — just went to the closet and started helping himself to the mister's things.

"That's when Joe got shot. He tried to make the army one stop doing it — and then the one with the hurt arm just up and took his pistol and killed Joe. He come for me right after that. I tried to run, get out of the house and hide in the field, but I tripped and fell. Was when he was picking me up that I seen the young one carrying Melly into the barn."

Callie Yarbro broke completely at that point, sat with head bowed while deep sobs shook her frail body. Gilmore appeared, hurrying along the street, bag in hand. He halted by the wagon, listened as Houston gave him a brief, hurried accounting, and then climbed up and found a place on the seat beside the girl, Melly. Arm around her, he began to soothe her, speaking now and then to the older woman.

Houston waited until Callie's weeping had subsided and then, standing next to Bryan, said: "Mrs. Yarbro, this is real important. When those outlaws rode off, did you see which way they went? I'm going after them and it will sure save me a lot of time if you can tell me which direction they took."

The woman's head came up and a fierceness came into her eyes. "North — they went north!" she said in a bitter voice. "Don't know where they was heading for, but they left our place going north. I hope you catch them, Deputy! I want to see all three of them swinging from a gibbet so's I can stand right there in front of them and laugh while they're adying! They ruined my girl, killed my mister — used me, and I want —"

Ben Houston pulled away as the woman's voice rose higher and higher. Gilmore shook his head warningly, indicating that the questioning had best end. The deputy nodded his understanding, drew Bryan aside.

"She said they headed north. Not much up that way for a lot of miles except Cheyenne — and it don't make sense they'd go anywhere near there. Could be a trick."

"Could be," the lawman agreed, "but trick or not it's all you've got to go on — so you best get started." His features were stiff and anger glowed in his eyes. "Now, I want you to stay after them till you've either got them jailed — or killed them — I ain't caring which."

"Could take a spell."

"No matter. When I see you next I want to hear you say you've done the job — and if you have you can figure on having my star. I know there's rumors of somebody else getting it, but I've still got some say-so around this town, and if the politicians don't see it my way, there's some closets where I can rattle a few bones that'll change their minds quick. You get them killers and the job's yours."

Determination and pride had welled up within Ben Houston. At last he was going to get the chance to prove himself and earn the badge he'd worked for so long. Squaring himself, he thrust out a hand to Bryan.

"Obliged to you, Sheriff. I'll get them — or I won't be back," he said and, wheeling, strode briskly to where his horses waited.

10

Despite fresh horses, traded for in a town near the Nebraska border, it had taken them almost a week to reach Buffalo City.

Mungor, furious at the way things had gone at the homestead where he had wanted only to purchase a meal and a few pieces of worn clothing, had lost no time in leaving the scene. He had led the party at a fast pace until they reached the first settlement, one called Carson Creek.

There, they made their presence known by loitering about the town's one saloon for a good half hour while all the time keeping a wary eye on the local lawman, an elderly constable, in the event he had been fore-warned and was inclined to act. But the man showed no particular interest in them, evidently not having received the word, and they finally departed, making it obvious they were continuing a course northward.

Once well away from Carson Creek,

however, and certain there was no one around to mark their passage, Mungor swung due east. He would be leaving the impression, he hoped, that they were riding to Wyoming, or possibly Montana, and by so doing throw the lawmen, whom he was sure were already in pursuit, off their trail.

Dressed entirely different from what they had been in Cheyenne and Denver, astride horses that did not resemble those used earlier, they turned into a small, southwest Kansas settlement and pulled up to the hitch rack of one of the numerous saloons that lined the busy street. The robbery in Denver had added a bit over eight thousand dollars to their poke and that did much to ease their mutual weariness and cool Mungor's smoldering anger at his partners for their actions at the Yarbro homestead.

"Jeez!" Sonny muttered, brushing at his nose. "Town stinks worse'n a slaughterhouse gut wagon! We holing up here?"

"Buffalo hides drying. You'll get used to it," Mungor replied, glancing about.

Buffalo City, a favorite haunt of hide hunters, offered nothing more than women, whiskey, and gambling. There was little in the way of accommodations, but it would be possible to find a place to sleep — and he felt it would be smart to drop out of sight for a few days, allow matters to cool off. He hadn't planned it that way — but Larch and Sonny pulling that damn fool stunt at Yarbro's —

Mungor, permitting his anger to subside, nodded to the younger man. "Something we'll have to do," he said, dismounting and tying his horse to the crossbar. Coming about he faced both men squarely. "Want you to hear this. I'm warning you for the last time. Another deal like back at that sod-buster's and I'll call it quits. Thanks to you, we've got the law hunting us now."

"Prob'ly are anyways," Larch said, reaching for his bottle. "How long you figure we could keep on running around holding up banks before they started looking for us?"

"Not saying they wouldn't start. They most likely did right after that mining company robbery. I'm saying they wouldn't work so hard at it if it wasn't no more than a holdup. But murder — and abusing a woman and a girl — that's something else! Law won't be letting that slide by."

"Well, it's done," Larch said, helping himself to a drink. He hesitated, looked off down the dusty street at the dozen or so men moving about, abruptly faced Mungor. "And while we're talking — I've got something to say. I'm mighty damn tired of you climbing on my back over something every time I turn around! I'm full growed and I reckon I'll do what I please — that plain?"

Mungor stiffened. Eyes narrowing he took a step toward the gunman. Immediately Sonny, silent during Larch's discharge of heated words, stepped in between them.

"Hell, there ain't no reason to have a falling out over something that's already been done," he said placatingly. "Was a mistake, doing what we did. I'll admit it and I expect Larch will — but we both was feeling mighty high after getting all that money and we just sort of celebrated too much. For me, I'm promising you it won't ever happen again."

The straight line of Mungor's shoulders broke, coming down slowly as the tautness left his rigid frame.

"It better not — not if you want to keep on adding cash to what we've got," he said in a less brittle voice. "Another stunt like that's bound to trip us up somewhere along the line and put an end to what we're doing."

"Well, we sure ain't going to be the cause of that, are we, Larch?" Sonny said, clapping the older man on the shoulder.

The stocky gunman favored Sonny with a disdainful look, downed another swallow from his bottle of whiskey, and headed for the entrance to the saloon which bore the sign on its front, THE PALACE. Sonny watched him briefly, then brought his attention back to Mungor.

"He'll be all right. I'll sort of see to it."

Mungor smiled; the thought of the younger man having any sort of influence or control over the hardcase struck him as amusing.

"Yeh, you do that," he said.

"We doing anything special while we're hanging around here?" Sonny, anxious, was striving to co-operate with Mungor and smooth over the rough spot over which they were passing.

"Nope, just watch your spending and don't do nothing that'll draw the law down on you. Can pass the word that we're horse buyers looking around for good stock. In a couple of days we'll take a fast ride up to Abilene and back. Bank up there that does a lot of business. Ought to be loaded with cash."

They moved in on the Abilene bank just at closing time, which, as Mungor had explained to his partners, was the ideal moment. Everything went like clockwork; the employees did as they were directed, and there were no interruptions from outsiders. Mungor emptied the safe of currency and gold, and then, since it sat in the area behind the teller's cage where it was in full view and not in a convenient closet, it was necessary they bind and gag the bank crew and leave them on the floor.

Making use of the card bearing the word CLOSED that hung near the door, they reversed it to face the street and, pulling the glass-centered panel shut, started a casual return to their horses, tethered to a tree in a nearby alley.

At that point Mungor's careful planning went awry. A shout went up in the street just beyond the bank. Mungor and his partners, wearing their gray slickers but with masks now pulled down and serving in their intended capacity as neckerchiefs, slowed, glanced over their shoulders. Two men, stars glinting on their vests, pistols in their hands, were hurrying toward them.

"Hold it!" one yelled.

"We've been spotted," Mungor muttered and broke into a run.

Gunshots sounded immediately. Dust began to kick up in the street nearby and ahead of them where bullets struck. Larch, keeping pace with Mungor and Sonny, drew his weapon, threw two quick shots at the lawmen.

"No!" Mungor yelled at the gunman. "You kill one of them and the fat's in the fire for sure!"

"Hell with that!" Larch replied. "Ain't no man going to shoot at me and I ain't shooting back!"

Mungor swore, hurried on. They reached the alley, veered into it. More men were now coming into the street, shouting, asking questions, and joining the lawmen in an impromptu posse.

Mungor, Sonny, and Larch, all sucking for breath, reached their horses, yanked the lines free, and vaulted onto their saddles.

"Going to be close!" Mungor warned as they cut about sharply. "We get separated — meet back at Buffalo City."

"Hell with that!" Larch said, crowding in close. "We're sticking together come brimstone or blizzard because you're carrying all the money — and you better be pulling that iron of yours and start using it or ain't none of us going nowhere!"

The two lawmen, reinforced now by half a dozen or more men, had gained the entrance to the alley. Mungor, with Larch at his side and Sonny a few yards ahead, spurred for the street at the opposite end of the passageway.

Guns opened up in earnest, filling the narrow alley with a thundering roll of echoes while bullets thudded into adjacent walls and roused dust about the hoofs of the onrushing horses from the bone-dry ground. Mungor drew his weapon, adding his shots to those of Larch. Sonny, taking his cue from the tall man, whipped out his pistol and then, together, all three laid down a return fire.

The lawmen and their volunteers slowed. The shooting fell off to a few scattered reports, and by the time Mungor and his partners had come to the street, it had all but ceased.

Grim, reloading as they raced on, now soaked with sweat, they swept out of the alley. A small group of men, additional volunteers apparently, had circled the block and were waiting. They opened up immediately. Mungor heard Sonny curse as a bullet nicked him somewhere, and then, bent low, pistols blasting, the three outlaws rode at full gallop directly at the crowd barring their way.

The volunteer lawmen scattered, stumbling and falling as they endeavored to get clear of the charging horses.

"Aim to teach them a lesson!" Larch shouted as they raced by. Leveling his pistol, he drew bead on one of the scurrying figures, barely visible through the swirling dust and drifting smoke.

"Don't!" Mungor yelled. "No need for another killing!"

Larch's dark face cracked into a mirthless grin. "The bastards can only hang me once!" he replied and pressed off a shot.

Mungor saw the man at whom Larch had aimed suddenly stiffen and go headlong to the ground. Anger flooded through him, and for an instant he had the urge to turn his weapon on the gunman — not because he had any particular aversion to another death — as Larch had said, they could be hanged only once no matter how many killings they had committed — but because the man was deliberately defying him and was thereby jeopardizing his carefully laid plans.

The friction between him and the gunman was growing more pronounced. He was beginning to wonder if the partnership could possibly survive until they reached the Mexican border.

He glanced back. The crowd, now well behind them, had been joined by the two lawmen and other volunteers. A group had gathered about the fallen man — but that would last for only moments; a mounted posse would be formed as soon as horses could be brought up.

"Keep going west!" Mungor shouted to Sonny, again half a dozen strides out in front. "Brush country there. Good chance we can lose them."

He didn't trouble to see if Larch had heard, or was even with them. One way or the other, he plain didn't give a damn.

11

"You all hear about what happened in Abilene?" the bartender asked.

Mungor, with Larch and Sonny, sitting at a table in the Palace Saloon, which had proven to be Buffalo City's finest, shook his head. "Not much. Was a robbery, wasn't it?"

They had returned to the settlement that morning, coming in from the south after ostensibly being on a trip during which they had looked over and contracted for a number of horses.

"Was a hell of a lot more'n that! Three jaspers rode in, held up the bank. Got away with more'n ten thousand dollars. Killed one of the lawmen that tried to stop them and shot up the town aplenty."

Mungor swore silently. It wasn't a lawman Larch had shot, but one of the local citizens who had taken a hand in the incident. And the amount of money the haul had netted was closer to eight thousand.

"They get the robbers?" Sonny wondered, beckoning to one of the saloon girls, a petite blonde in an ankle-length, low-cut dress. He had just been to the barber for a shave and a liberal application of lilac water.

"No, hadn't last I heard. Had a good start on the marshal and his posse and lost them in the brush country. I've been told that —"

The garrulous bartender paused, glanced at the counter where a customer had materialized, and crossed to serve the man's wants. The blonde had reached the table in response to Sonny's summons and now stood at his side smiling widely as she looked down at him. Around them the evening's activities were being prepared for — swampers lighting the lamps, straightening up tables and chairs, sweeping and doing all the other minor things necessary.

Other women were making an appearance, coming in through the rear door from the small shacks behind the saloon that served as living quarters. The piano player, an elderly man in stained duck pants of the type sailors wore, collarless shirt closed at the neck with a copper button, and a black banjo accompanist whose skin shone darkly in the yellow light, had already taken their places at one end of the small, dirt-floor area set aside for dancing.

Dust and smoke were already beginning to gather in motionless clouds beneath the low roof, all but obscuring the walls which bore numerous mounted animal heads and, in a display of grim, tasteless humor, that of an Indian chief, separated by a saw from its wooden body, affixed to a circular plaque, and hung along with the other trophies of the hunt.

"What I was saying," the bartender resumed, returning after the interruption, "was that folks up there think that bunch was part of the James gang — that they've probably quit Jesse and Frank and've shoved off on their own."

"They got any idea which ones they are?" Mungor asked.

"Nope. All was wearing masks and long overcoats, so there wasn't nobody got a good look at them. There's talk of calling in the Pinkerton Agency, putting a detective on their trail. Abilene's plenty riled up over it."

"Can't blame them," Mungor said, watching Sonny rise and move off toward the rear door of the saloon with the blonde in tow. The small bloodstain on his pant leg where a bullet had nicked him during the escape at Abilene was clearly noticeable.

Mungor shrugged in disgust. Sonny

should have burned the pants, put on another pair that in no way could link him — and them — to the shooting in Abilene. It would be a thoughtless bit of carelessness such as that which could trip them up and send them all to the gallows one day.

The bartender had retired to his counter and was now busy with half a dozen customers. Larch, tossing off a drink and immediately refilling his glass from the bottle before him on the table, raised his level, hooded glance to Mungor. They had barely spoken to each other since Abilene.

"That jasper weren't no lawman," he said. "Was just some counterjumper."

"We're getting credit for killing a lawman just the same," Mungor replied coldly. "Being so damned handy with that pistol of yours is going to make it tougher for us to keep on."

Larch's thick shoulders moved. "Just because you're chickenhearted about triggering that iron you're wearing don't mean me and the kid have to be the same."

Mungor's face darkened. If he didn't need Larch to continue with his scheme, or if they weren't so deeply involved in theft and murder together, he'd rid himself of the gunman then and there and go it alone with Sonny; but Larch was a man he could not do without and bringing in another, a stranger, to replace him was out of the question.

"Time comes when it's necessary, I'll use my gun," he said, raising his voice to be heard above the mounting din.

Over in the dance area several couples were stomping out a hoedown — a few of the men with women, others with bewhiskered partners like themselves. Larch stared at the lunging figures for a long minute, again had a drink, and came back to Mungor.

"Way I see it, not being scared to do some shooting's all in our favor. Word'll get around fast that bucking us is a good way to die quick, and that'll make it easier for us 'cause they'll be right anxious to do just what we tell them to do."

Mungor took up his glass, finished its fiery contents. "Have it your way, Larch — but it's a big mistake. I aim to see the end of this and go ahead with the plans I've got for enjoying the rest of my life in Mexico. Doubt if you'll ever even make it to the border if you keep on killing."

The gunman tossed off another drink. "And you will, eh?"

"I will," Mungor replied with no qualification.

Larch brushed at his lips. "Well, me and the kid'll get there, too — don't go thinking we won't. And it'll probably be my gun that'll do it for us. . . . You believing any about what that bartender said — the people up in Abilene calling in the Pinkerton outfit?"

"Probably true," Mungor replied, his voice still stiff. "Somebody's bound to sooner or later. Banks start getting robbed and when the local law can't seem to do anything about it, that's who they bring in."

"It going to change anything for us?"

"Nothing — far as I'm concerned."

"Good. We going to hole up here for a spell, or are we pulling out again? Country's kind of riled up, way that bartender talks."

"That'll be around Abilene. Well be hitting Emporia next. Nobody'll be looking for us to show up down there."

Larch grinned, again brushed at his mouth. "Hate to tell you this, but you sure are something!" he said grudgingly, and then added cheerfully, "But I reckon if you wasn't, I'd've blowed your head off weeks ago! When we pulling out?"

"First thing in the morning. Can drop the word that we're going back to Texas and pick up those horses we bought. Soon as we're out of sight, we'll head for Emporia.

Bank there'll be worth a few thousand."

Mungor got to his feet. "Best we all be turning in. If you see Sonny before I do, tell him we'll be riding at first light and to get some sleep. Goes for you, too."

Larch swore, wagged his head. "There you go ordering me around again! I reckon you don't learn no better'n me."

"Suit yourself —"

"Just what I aim to do," Larch said, casting a speculative eye on one of the saloon girls facing him with a questioning smile. "Ain't no sense having a pocketful of cash if you don't spend some of it having yourself a good time. . . . The kid's got the right idea — does his sleeping in the saddle."

"Could be," Mungor said, watching the gunman rise and join the girl.

After a bit he headed for the door. Maybe Sonny and Larch did have the right slant — but for now he'd keep his sights set on Mexico.

The Emporia bank robbery was little different from the one in Denver; there were no complications during or afterward, and they rode out with no one except the employees aware of what had taken place.

Halting a few hours later in a brushy hollow to rest the horses, Mungor followed his usual custom of counting the take; it turned out to be almost seven thousand dollars.

Sonny slapped his thigh, laughed appreciatingly. "That there whomps the total up to near thirty thousand, don't it?"

"About twenty-nine," Mungor said, storing the bills and coins into the canvas sack. It was beginning to bulge and the weight was considerable.

He wished he could stash the money somewhere for safekeeping until they reached the figure they had set as a goal but could think of no place where it would be readily available when the time came to cross the border.

"Where we going now — back to Buffalo City?" Larch, nursing his bottle of whiskey, asked. The delicate truce existing between him and Mungor was still holding, both men apparently walking soft so as to not cause an open and final break.

"No, we've pushed our luck there far as it's safe to," the tall man replied. "Goes for these slickers, too — let's scoop out a hole here in the sand and bury them. And it'll be a good idea to swap horses and change clothes again."

"You got some town in mind where we can do all that without bringing the law down on us?" the gunman wondered, his tone faintly sarcastic.

"Joplin — across the line in Missouri. Doubt if they've heard about the robberies yet. We can outfit ourselves and clean out the bank while we're there."

12

"Trouble with the miners," Mungor said, when he returned to the abandoned shack at the edge of Joplin where they had established their base. "Don't know for sure what it's all about, and I figured asking a lot of questions wouldn't be smart — but the town's shut down tight."

They had reached the settlement just across the Missouri border around noon that day. As was the custom, Mungor rode in alone to have a look and refresh his memory of the settlement before any move was made.

"That mean we're passing up the place?" Larch asked. He was hunched on his heels, back to the wall of the old house, his bottle of whiskey in one hand, a cigar in the other.

Mungar stared out across the low, rolling hills, turned vivid here and there by thickets of sassafras and persimmon. "Far as the bank's concerned we'll have to," he said.

"Could find us a general store around somewheres. Ought to be good for a few hundred dollars," the gunman suggested.

Sonny, dozing nearby in the warm sun, stirred, sat up. "That ain't nothing but chicken feed, and not worth bothering with."

Larch shook his head angrily, took a turn at his whiskey bottle. "The hell with that! I ain't making that ride down here from Emporia just for shucks!"

"You won't be," Mungor said evenly. "Well go ahead getting new clothes and fresh horses like we planned. There'll be a store open somewhere, probably at the other end of town — and a livery stable, too."

Sonny, on his feet, was smiling broadly. "I aim to get myself one of the big white hats like I seen —"

"You best forget that, buy something that won't be so noticeable," Mungor interrupted. "Might as well wear a red flag. Everybody around will recollect seeing you."

Sonny's head dropped in disappointment and his face sobered. "Yeh, reckon you're right."

"What we're needing is plain clothes — nothing that will stick in folks' minds if they're asked to give a description. And this time instead of slickers we'll get dust coats — the long, tan-colored ones. Just about everybody in Kansas wears one, I noticed. We best split up and get at it now. All of us showing up at one place buying whole new outfits just might start people to wondering."

"That mean you're wanting us to split up, leave you alone with all the money?" Larch demanded, eyes narrowing.

"Exactly what I mean," Mungor replied coolly and waited for further words from the gunman. When they did not come, he continued: "Get your new duds and do your horse trading and come back here. Don't pull something that'll put the law on your tail — act like you're a cowhand just fixing yourself up. Figured to meet about dark. . . . You got any objections, Larch?"

The heavy-set man spat into the dust. "I sure do! I don't like trusting you with —"

"Hell, Mungor ain't going to run off with our money!" Sonny exclaimed. "Knows we'd be right on his trail if he tried it."

"Maybe so, but why not me taking care of it instead of him? I can look after it same as he's doing."

Sonny grinned. "Now, don't be taking this personal, Larch, but I don't figure I can trust you like I can him."

The gunman's features hardened and a glint came into his eyes as he stared at the smiling Sonny. And then, anger fading, he shrugged, came upright.

"Oh, the hell with it," he said and shifted his attention to Mungor. "I'll be doing like you say, mister, but if you ain't here time I get back, you can figure on me breathing down your neck for the rest of your life till I catch up with you! You hear me?"

"I'll be here — by dark," Mungor said in his quiet, even way. "And soon as we're back together and set, we'll move out."

"For where?" Sonny asked.

"Wichita — it's only a couple of days from here."

Larch's attitude suddenly changed, and his heavy features came alive with interest. "Wichita — that's a hell of a good town! Pretty good size, too; we won't find the banks all locked up there no matter what's going on."

Mungor studied the gunman closely. "You know the place good?"

"Sure — leastwise, some of it. Know other towns in Kansas, too — Larned, Hays, a couple more."

A half-smile cracked Mungor's lips. "How's it happen you never mentioned it?"

"You never asked me nothing about it —

and you ain't one to take advice kindly. I done quite a spell of riding up through there."

"Glad to hear it," Mungor said dryly. "Just might call on you for some help — someday."

Deputy Ben Houston pulled up at the makeshift livery stable at the south end of Buffalo City and waited for the hostler to come to him from the far side of the corral. The stench of hides drying in the sun still hung over the settlement in a gut-wrenching cloud just as it had the time previous when he visited there, and he reckoned the hide business was still good despite the slaughter that had long since decimated the herds of buffalo.

He had gone north following the three outlaws, who had robbed the Denver bank and then compounded their crime with rape and murder, tracing them through the village of Carson Creek, after which he lost the trail.

Later he had doubled back, finally encountering a farm hand who had noticed three riders headed east in a hurry. He realized the killers had been playing it safe, apparently knowing that a posse, or at least a lawman, would be searching for them.

Continuing east, Houston picked up definite proof at a town near the Nebraska border where they had traded horses and further outfitted themselves with new clothing. It was there that he'd lost all trace of the party.

On a hunch he swung south into Kansas, heading for Buffalo City — a wild, wide-open town that was a favored hangout of outlaws as well as hide-hunters — arriving there just before dark. He'd gone directly to one of the several livery stables, where, logically, the outlaws would have stabled their horses — assuming they had stopped there.

"Yeh?" the stablekeeper greeted him as he wiped sweat off his brow with a grimy hand.

Houston, his star prudently out of sight in a shirt pocket, shifted on the saddle. "Aim to spend the night. You look after my horses?"

"What I'm in business for," the hostler said irritably.

"Give them some grain along with plenty of fresh hay. Go easy on the water —"

"What the hell? You think I'm some kind of a greenhorn that don't know how to look after stock?" the stableman demanded, hitching at his stained trousers. "Mister, you can just take your damned horses and go —"

"This place'll do fine," the deputy cut in,

smiling. "Thought maybe I had to ask for grain."

"Well, you do — and it costs aplenty around here," the hostler replied, mollified.

"No matter, take care of them. You want your pay now or in the morning when I pull out?"

"Morning's all right."

Houston nodded, started to turn away, and then, as if an afterthought, came back around. "Looking for some friends of mine — three men. Would've rode in several days ago, if they came this way. Tall fellow, a kid, and short, heavy-set fellow."

"Sure, I seen them. Horse traders. Hung out at the Palace Saloon."

"They still around?"

"Don't know for certain. Ain't seen them for a spell — they been keeping their horses in that barn back of the saloon. Best you go on to the Palace, talk to Jake, the bartender. He got sort of friendly with them."

"Obliged," Houston said, masking his elation, and, pivoting, moved off down the dusty street restless with traffic.

He found the Palace, the largest among the many saloons, near the center of the settlement, and entered. Halting just within the smoke-filled room long enough for his eyes to adjust, he glanced about, saw no group of three men who fitted the description of the outlaws and, crossing to the bar, ordered a drink.

"You Jake?" he asked as he was being served.

The bartender nodded. "Who wants to know?"

"Name's Ben," Houston said, making a show of being evasive. "Looking for some friends — was told you might know where they are. Three men — a tall fellow, a kid —"

"Ain't they got no names?"

"Plenty, and it'd be hard to tell which ones they're using. Could be doing some horse trading."

"Oh, you're talking about Mungor and Larch, and Sonny — that's what the kid's calling hisself."

Houston smiled. "That'll be them. Used them same names before. They around somewheres?"

A small, blond girl dressed in a red, full-length dress swaggered up. Head cocked prettily to one side, she smiled.

"Who's your friend, Jake? Don't recollect seeing him around here before."

The bartender shrugged indifferently. "Says his name's Ben. Looking for Mungor and the others. . . . Allie was real friendly with Sonny," Jake added, again addressing Houston. "Reckon she can tell you what you want to know better'n anybody."

The bartender moved off to wait on another customer. Allie, continuing to smile, said, "You a friend of Sonny's?"

"Can say that, I guess —"

"He sure is a case, ain't he?"

"For a fact," the lawman agreed. "You know where I can find him?"

The girl eased up to the bar, helped herself to the remaining liquor in Houston's glass. "No, sure don't. They was here a few days, then one morning they was gone."

Houston digested that bit of disappointing information with no change of expression. "Got any idea which way they headed? I'm in a powerful hurry to join up with them."

Allie shook her head. "Nope, sure ain't — Sonny never said nothing about where they was going — or even that they was leaving. He never did talk much about things like that, where he come from or where he was going, I mean. Did tell me that time him and the others was going down into Texas to do some horse trading."

"Did they?"

"Yeh, was gone three or four days."

"That the only time they left here?"

Allie frowned, studied Ben Houston suspiciously. "You ain't talking much like a friend — more like a stinking badge-toter —"

Houston beckoned to Jake, motioned for him to refill his glass and provide one for the girl. Smiling at her, he said: "Been a long time since I last seen them. Just trying to catch up on what they're doing nowadays."

Allie nodded, accepting the explanation, and downed her drink, glanced over her shoulder. "Reckon I best get busy — trade's picking up," she said. "Sure obliged to you, Ben, for the drink, and I wish I could help you. That Sonny was a real generous fellow. Tell him that for me when you see him."

"Sure will," Houston replied absently, his thoughts now centering on the few days that Mungor and the others had been absent from Buffalo City — supposedly buying horses. Odds were that was merely a cover-up for another robbery somewhere. Taking up his drink he tossed it off, grinned at Jake.

"Well, if I missed Sonny and them, I've missed them — and there ain't no use sweating about it. I been over the Colorado country — high mountains. Like living in another world — man never sees nobody or hears about anything. What's been going on

114

around here?"

"Big talk of the railroad coming," Jake said, helping himself to a drink. "And the James gang's running wild again."

"Jesse and Frank James?"

"Yep, leastwise, folks thinks it's part of their gang. Three of them robbed the Abilene bank the other day, been a week or more now. Got a lot of money and shot a lawman."

Three men . . . Abilene bank . . . a week or so ago. It added up. Ben Houston placed his empty glass on the bar and turned away. He'd be willing to bet his last dollar that he'd picked up the killers' trail again.

13

"There's the bank," Mungor said, pointing at a narrow-fronted frame building on the opposite side of the street.

With Larch and Sonny, he was standing in the shadows that filled what had once been a livery barn but, gutted at some time in the past by fire, was now only an empty shell.

"Plenty quiet, seems," Sonny observed, rubbing at the stubble on his chin.

"This ain't the main part of Wichita," Larch said, taking his bottle of whiskey from a pocket and pulling the cork. "This here's a little bank. There ain't going to be much in it."

"Be enough," Mungor said evenly. "Going down into the middle of town where the main one is would not only be risky, but stupid."

Larch shrugged, took a drink. The sky overhead, visible through a gaping, jagged hole in the roof of the ravaged structure, was a brilliant blue as the rays of the descending sun flooded it.

"Would be worth it," the gunman continued, stubbornly.

"If we got away with it."

Again Larch's shoulders stirred. "Ain't going to get nothing here but chicken feed."

Mungor's jaw hardened at the senseless wrangling, but he restrained his temper and rode out a long minute. They were all wearing their new clothing — pants, shirts, neckerchiefs, hats, and long, tan dusters. In no way did they fit the descriptions that had been passed along by previous victims other than size and the fact they were three in number.

"We'll split up," Mungor said, shifting the saddlebags, which had become heavier steadily, to a more comfortable position on his shoulder. "You two drop back, come up on the other side of the street. I'll wait till you're close, then cross over and reach the bank a couple of steps ahead of you. I'll turn in same as if I was there to do some business. You follow me close."

"How about the masks?" Sonny asked.

"Like always — when you get inside and before anybody gets a look at you, pull them up into place. And shut the door — this

117

time of day it'll look natural." Mungor paused, looked directly at Larch. "I don't want any shooting, not unless we get backed into a corner. This town's got some good lawmen."

The gunman said something under his breath. Mungor considered him silently for a brief time, waiting to see if the man intended to make his comments audible. When it appeared he did not, the tall man shifted his attention again to the bank. Although there was much activity farther down the street in the direction of the town's center, no one had departed or entered the structure.

"Let's get at it," Mungor said and started toward the corner of the charred, old barn.

Reaching there he halted, glanced at Sonny and Larch. Walking casually, they were in the act of crossing the street. Little spurts of dust rose from beneath their boots each time a step was taken. He watched them gain the board sidewalk on the opposite side, turn, head for the bank, paying no attention to the two intervening stores, a meat market and a saddlery, during their passage.

Mungor nodded in satisfaction. Both Larch and Sonny had learned to carry out their parts well, neither betraying any special interest in their surroundings, doing nothing to attract attention, and giving anyone noting their presence the impression they were merely two riders in off the range and in town to see the elephant.

It was time for him to make his move. Sliding his saddlebags down to where they hung across his forearm, Mungor stepped out of the shadows into the open, walked a short distance on that near side of the street, then angled across to the bank. To anyone observing, he was a man, money or papers in the leather bags he was carrying, going to the establishment for the purpose of conducting business.

He reached the door two steps ahead of Larch and Sonny, cast a side glance at them. The gunman's features wore their usual stolid scowl; Sonny was grinning slightly as if in anticipation of the haul they would make. He winked when Mungor caught his eye.

There were no customers in the bank, now in the process of closing for the day. Face tipped down, Mungor halted in the center of the small lobby, seemingly unsure of just whether to patronize the lone teller standing behind his wire-fronted cage, or one of the two men seated at tables close by. One glanced up, frowning as if irritated that a customer should arrive so near to closing time.

"Something I can do for you?" he asked, pushing the green eyeshade he was wearing higher on his forehead. Abruptly his mouth sagged as he caught sight of Larch and Sonny standing beyond Mungor. His eyes spread wide and he came to his feet slowly.

"It's them!" he gasped. "That bunch from the James gang!"

Mungor, mask in place, glanced to a room in the rear that adjoined the lobby where still another man sat at a desk reading. As the sound of Sonny closing the door to the street reached him, he nodded to Larch, pointed to the side room, drawing his attention to the fourth member of the bank crew, and came back to the others.

"Not here to hurt any of you," he said quietly. "Just aiming to clean out your safe. Now, I want you all in there — with the boss," he added, pointing with his pistol.

"And don't go trying something brave," Larch added. "We ain't shooting nobody unless we have to."

The man in the inner office, elderly, dressed in a gray suit, stiff collar, black tie, and wearing steel-rimmed spectacles, had risen, was looking toward his employees, a puzzled expression on his face as they filed into the room. Impulsively, he came out from behind his desk, started toward the door.

"Back inside, Grandpa," Larch said, waving him back. "We've come to take all your money."

The man retreated a step or two, shock blanking his features. Then, "It's the James gang!" he blurted, echoing his employee. "It's them!"

"It sure is," Larch said as the last of the crew passed into the room. "Now, you all behave unless you want one of us Jameses to kill you."

Mungor had turned for the safe as the gunman's laconic warning reached him. He glanced to the bank's entrance. Sonny had not only shut the door but pulled down the green roller shade that announced the establishment was closed for the day. The younger man grinned, and he hurried on to the vault.

Reaching it, Mungor quickly stripped it of its stacks of currency and gold, ignoring, as was his custom, the silver. Placing the money in one of the bank's own canvas bags which he found handy, the tall man crossed to the teller's cage, collected the currency and gold coins he found there, and doubled hurriedly back to the center of the room.

Gun in hand, arms folded across his chest, Larch was awaiting him, a hard, dry smile on his lips. He ducked his head at the adjoining office where the employees and the bank owner were now prisoners behind a locked door.

"We're waiting on you," the gunman said.

"Not any longer," Mungor replied and headed for the building's entrance.

Sonny at once opened the panel, threw a searching glance up and down the street.

"Woman coming," he announced, and then added: "Nope, turned into that butcher shop. We leaving together?"

Mungor said, "Sure — only take it slow. We've just done some business here. No need to hurry."

They left the bank, crossed the street leisurely, and entered the old livery stable. Once inside Mungor pivoted, again examined the now-darkening lane. There was no one in sight, and, of course, no activity in front of the bank. He nodded to Sonny and Larch, a wave of exultation and pride surging through him.

"Pulled that one off slick as a gut!" he said as they hurried now to reach their horses at the opposite end of the barn.

"For sure!" Sonny declared. "The law'll be running around like a bunch of chickens with their heads cut off! I just can't get over how easy doing this is."

They came to the horses, pulled the tie ropes free and swung up onto their saddles. Mungor, exhilaration still gripping him, sending the blood racing through his body, nodded to his partners.

"We still take it slow," he said and they cut into the alley behind the stable. "No cause to rush. Be an hour or two before anybody finds out what happened and gets a posse mounted — to go hunting for the James gang."

Sonny laughed. Larch permitted himself a grin. "Sure did go nice — I got to say it. Where we heading for next?"

Mungor, looking straight ahead as they loped lazily down the road, could not resist congratulating himself. He was feeling good — great, in fact. Every deal had gone pretty much as planned and they were rapidly growing richer while the lawmen, as Sonny had noted, were running wildly about getting nowhere. Well, he'd make them look even bigger fools!

"Larned," he said. "Not far from here. We'll get there fast, strip the bank, and be gone while the law's still beating the bushes around Wichita for us."

Sonny slapped his thigh, laughed. Larch

shrugged, took a turn at his bottle.

"That suits me right down to a nub," he said. "I got a right special reason to get even with that burg."

14

It was a long trip for the horses, and a hard one, but they reached the outskirts of Larned around dusk of the following day. Mungor was still flushed with success, reveling in the remembrance of how easily they had extracted six thousand dollars from the Wichita bank, anxious to increase the take while having a good laugh at the frantic and futile efforts of the lawmen who were endeavoring to run them down.

Larned was a fair little town; he saw that as he viewed a faded sign erected at the end of the street bearing the admonition: DON'T WEAR YOUR GUN!

"I hear you say you know this place?" he said, turning to Larch. He doubted they would come away from such a small settlement with much to show for their efforts, but it was important to him that they strike again — simply to further embarrass the law.

The gunman nodded, tucked his near-empty bottle of whiskey back into the pocket of his jacket. "Reckon so."

"Where's the bank?"

"Ain't got one — leastwise didn't use to."

Mungor swore. Since he had chosen to pull a holdup in Larned on an impulse, it wasn't one of the places he had previously scouted and made definite plans for.

"People've got to keep their money somewhere," he said. "Doubt if they'd be chancing a sugar bowl."

Larch scrubbed at his jaw. "Well, them that's got any to keep, prob'ly turn it over to old man McGowan to keep. Runs the general store — leastwise, he did."

"Reckon he's still doing it," Sonny said. "I can see it from here — big place near the end of the street. What's that there flat-topped thing, Larch? Looks like a fort."

"The jail," the gunman muttered. "Can tell you all about it. Was put in there once."

"Looks like it's made of wood?"

"Just what it is — but might as well be iron. It's like being throwed into a hole in the ground and then covered over. Hardly any breathing air or light. Time they put me in there, they most forget all about doing it."

"What's that place next to McGowan's?"

Mungor said, his eyes again traveling Larned's near-deserted street.

"Reckon you could call it a hotel. Saloon there beside it's called the Plainsman, or was last time I was here."

"That's where we'll put up for the night," Mungor said. "Horses'll have to rest good before we can use them again. Something else — when you stable them, pay the bill. Won't have time in the morning — and we don't want no hostler doing a lot of yelling and stirring up the law for a couple of dollars."

"You aiming to clean out this here McGowan's store?" Sonny asked.

"What we came here for," Mungor said irritably. He had assumed there would be a bank and was being compelled to settle for a small-time store; it was dulling the edge of his newly acquired vanity.

"When?"

"Morning, first thing. We'll get ourselves rooms at the hotel — doing it one at a time, like always, because we don't want to be seen together. Goes for the livery stable, too. Then, come first light, we'll get the horses and meet in back of McGowan's. Clear?"

"Sure is," Sonny said, now anxious to reach the saloon where he could see several garishly dressed women lounging about the entrance.

Mungor placed his glance on Larch. He was recalling what the gunman had said about owing the town and a vague tag of worry was plucking at his mind.

"What about you — you underst —"

"Hell, yes, I savvy!" the gunman snapped. "You think I'm ten years old or something?"

"Seemed you wasn't paying no mind," Mungor said quietly. "I don't want no slip-ups."

Larch glared at the tall man. "Meaning?"

Sonny, unable to restrain himself longer, began to pull away. "I'll get signed in first," he said.

Mungor did not shift his attention from the gunman. "Meaning I don't want somebody stirring up trouble and hoodooing the job in the morning —"

"Can look after myself," Larch said stiffly, and abruptly spurring his horse, he moved off toward the center of the settlement.

Mungor saw no more of either partner after that until later in the evening at the Plainsman. He had registered in at the hotel, cleaned up, and, after hiding the canvas bags of money inside his cornshuck mattress, had treated himself to a big meal of steak and potatoes with all the trimmings and then made his way to the saloon.

Night was complete and lamps glowed in the windows of the residences along with a few, including McGowan's, of the business houses. Mungor stood for a time in the darkness beside one of the structures, having a thorough look at the store, a large, sprawling structure built up off the ground as if floodwater was expected.

The building had a door and a small window in the front, even smaller windows in the sides. The rear, he saw while strolling casually into that direction later, had only a door which opened out onto a loading platform.

Studying the place for a time, Mungor decided it would not be difficult to rob; the smallness of the windows made observation from the street an impossibility, so he need not worry over being seen by passersby. What did trouble him was just where McGowan kept the money — his and that deposited with him by the townspeople.

The answer to the question was of vital importance, one best not left until morning as time then would be critical. Accordingly Mungor, continuing his stroll, moved on down the street until he reached the half-dozen steps that led up to the platform fronting the store, mounted them, and entered.

A middle-aged man came forward to meet him. There were no other patrons, Mungor saw, and noted also in his swift survey of the large square room that McGowan evidently had living quarters in the rear.

"Something you're needing?"

Mungor nodded. "Cigars."

The storekeeper pointed to a counter with a curved glass top. "Right over there," he said, and stepped around behind it.

Mungor, eyes now searching for a safe, or the indication of a vault of some sort, followed McGowan to the display case. Indicating a box of well-known stogies, he gathered half a dozen in his hand, when the storekeeper opened the case, and reached into a pocket for money.

"Be a quarter," McGowan said, closing the display. "Nickel each, six for a quarter."

"Cheap enough," Mungor commented and, passing the coin to the man, turned to go.

"Sure there ain't something else?" the merchant called after him. "I'm about to lock up for the night."

Mungor hesitated, glanced back. McGowan had added the quarter to a tin box which he now was placing alongside several other similar containers inside a cabinet that stood behind the rear counter. A hasp and thick padlock secured the door.

"No," Mungor said, continuing on his way. "This will do it. Good night."

"G'night," McGowan answered.

Back on the deserted street, Mungor thrust one of the weeds into his mouth, lit it, and bent his steps toward the Plainsman. Light was pouring from its open front door and windows, along with the steady rumble of voices, peals of laughter, and the faint tinkling of a piano.

Entering, he crossed to the bar, flicking Larch, who was leaning against the lower end of the counter, with his glance.

He called for whiskey when one of the bartenders stepped up to serve him, and after paying and taking up the thick-bottomed shot glass, came about. Resting against the counter, he surveyed the smoke-filled room with half-closed eyes. He was feeling good — satisfied; he knew where McGowan kept the cash, and getting it would be fairly simple.

He saw Sonny at that moment. The younger man, a girl on each arm, entered the saloon from a rear door. They were laughing and talking noisily as they angled across the fairly crowded floor to the area near the piano that was set aside for dancing. Sonny, he reckoned, was making up for the few days and nights when they were on the move and there were no women available.

He could use a bit of female company himself. The last time was weeks ago, he reckoned — back in Cheyenne. Mungor brought his attention back to the bar, dropping the stogie, for which he had no taste, into the brass cuspidor at his feet. Larch had purchased a quart bottle of whiskey, was moving off into the crowd, his steps deliberate and steady. Like as not he was headed for his room where he would sit quietly alone and swill the liquor until sleep finally overcame him.

Mungor became aware that he was being observed closely by one of the saloon girls, a slender brunette in yellow, with large, wide-set eyes and a friendly smile. He nodded, pointed to one of the few tables not in use. The girl immediately started toward it. Mungor motioned to the bartender.

"Bring us a bottle and a couple of glasses," he said, indicating where he would be, and crossed to where the girl in yellow had taken a chair and was awaiting him.

"Name's Charity," she said brightly as he sat down opposite her. "What'll I call you?"

"John's as good as any," he replied, giving her a false name for no reason other than it seemed a good idea.

"John it is," the girl said and leaned back as the bartender arrived with Mungor's order. After he had set it on the table, collected his money, and withdrawn, she fell to studying Mungor again. "I don't remember seeing you in here before," she said, finally.

"I'm sort of in and out," he replied non-committally, pouring the drinks.

The racket in the Plainsman had increased to a near-deafening level. Several of the customers were attempting to sing, and the dozen or so couples on the plank dance floor were stamping lustily to the tune the piano player was pounding out. Smoke was a heavy blue fog overhead, its sharp odor mingling with that of spilled liquor and sweaty bodies.

"You want to dance?" Charity asked, tossing off her drink.

Mungor's eyes were on Sonny, beating out a step of some kind with one of his girls. He shook his head. "Not what I had in mind —"

Charity laughed and, glass still in hand, got to her feet. "Come on, then — we're wasting time."

Mungor grinned, rose. He liked a woman

who didn't dilly-dally around. Picking up the bottle and his glass, he turned, started to follow the girl to the door in the rear of the saloon, paused as a man came rushing in through the front, yelling.

"Anybody seen the marshal? Some jasper set fire to the jail!"

"He burn it down?" one of the barkeeps asked, as a crowd quickly gathered.

"Nope — some of us seen him doing it, got it put out before it done any damage. The marshal —"

"Who was it done it — one of the prisoners?"

"Nope. Fellow was on the outside."

"Outside!" a voice in the gathering echoed.

"What I said. Can't figure out why he'd do it. There ain't nobody inside right now, so he sure weren't trying to get somebody out."

"You know who he is?"

"Stranger to me. Short, heavy-set man — mean-looking as a bucket of scalded snakes. Was in here a bit ago buying himself a bottle."

Anger roared suddenly through Mungor. It would be that damned Larch! He should have known that the gunman, with something sticking crosswise in his craw, would get himself into trouble of some kind.

"Where's he now?"

"Hell, we couldn't do nothing but shove him inside and lock the door. Figured that was what the marshal'd want us to do."

"Expect so," someone said. "He drunk?"

"Had that quart bottle on him — was about half full."

"He was mighty drunk then. Can't no man guzzle that much whiskey that fast and still stay sober —"

Mungor came half about, the smell of lilac water reaching him above all the other odors filling the saloon. Sonny, a girl hanging on each arm, was staring at him. The question was plain in his eyes — hadn't they better go help Larch, get him out of the dungeon-like prison that he hated so fiercely?

The tall man shook his head, turned to Charity. Let the gunman lay out the remainder of the night inside the wooden jail. He'd not get himself in any more trouble, locked away as he was. When first light came, he and Sonny would release him.

Taking Charity's hand, he followed her across the saloon for the door in the rear that led outside.

15

Mungor, his horse as well as Larch's saddled, the pry bar he had procured from the livery stable's smithy in his hand, waited impatiently for Sonny to show. Light streaks were already breaking the dark eastern horizon, and the need to force an entry into McGowan's store, empty the cashboxes, and hasten on to the jail and release Larch before the settlement began to stir, was urgent.

But he had no one to fault but himself, Mungor thought. Larned was a town he'd not scouted and therefore was not in his plans; he had gone there on impulse — as a sop to his personal vanity, in reality. He'd not again vary from his original list of predetermined victims — not for any reason.

The scrape of a boot heel on the sun-baked ground brought Mungor to an alert. Sonny, hat pulled down over his face, a belted pistol hanging from a shoulder, emerged from the gloom.

"You're late," Mungor said in a gruff voice.

Sonny shrugged, stepped up to Larch's horse, and hung the extra cartridge belt and weapon on the saddle. In the weak light coming from a lantern suspended in the runway, he appeared somewhat drawn.

"Got halfway here, remembered Larch wouldn't have his gun. Went back to his room for it."

Mungor grunted. "Glad you thought of it," he said, his manner relenting.

Sonny, working fast but carefully, threw gear onto his horse. "Larch is sure going to be riled up — us leaving him locked in that jailhouse all night."

"Let him. Was the best thing — him feeling the way he does about this town."

"Never knowed him to get so much liquor inside him that he'd try a fool stunt like that —"

"Wasn't that. Whiskey never affects him much. It's that he's got something against this place. Would've probably tried to burn down the whole town if he'd managed to get the jail going. Locked up was the safest place for him to be. . . . You about ready? We're running late —"

For answer, Sonny backed his horse out of its stall. Noting the length of iron with its tapered end that Mungor was holding, he said: "That what we're using to pry open the jail door?"

Mungor nodded. "After we get through at McGowan's," he replied and led his horse and that of Larch's through the doorway into the pale darkness outside.

"You figuring on just me and you robbing that store?" Sonny asked, catching up.

"All we'll need. I looked the place over last night. Job'll be a cinch," Mungor said and detailed what he had learned about the store earlier. "We get in, you stand watch at the door leading into McGowan's living quarters — couldn't tell last night if there was a way to lock it or not — while I go through the deposit boxes he's got in that cabinet."

"Might take awhile if they're locked —"

"That won't be no chore with a thick-bladed skinning knife, and there's a whole caseful of them real handy."

The front door of McGowan's yielded quickly and fairly quietly to the bar Mungor had provided. Inside he indicated the entrance to the storekeeper's quarters. Weapon in hand, Sonny crossed hurriedly, took up a stand there. Since it was still early and no one was yet abroad, and seeing through the windows from the street was almost an impossibility, Mungor felt it was unnecessary to guard against any interruption from that direction.

He wasted no time getting down to work. Selecting a heavy knife from the display case, Mungor opened the cabinet and, with further aid from the thick-bladed Green River, broke the locks of the metal containers and swiftly emptied them onto a nearby counter.

It was too dark to distinguish much of what he was finding, and striking a match would be risky; but the feel of currency as opposed to folds of papers and pieces of jewelry and keepsakes was not difficult.

Taking a paper sack from the stack on the counter, he collected the bills, ignoring all else, and stuffed them into it. The take was going to be small, hardly worth the effort, he realized, but they had gone this far and it would be foolish to leave empty-handed. Besides, the whole idea had been to further mock the lawmen beating the brush for them around Wichita.

The bag stuffed inside his shirt, Mungor dropped back to Sonny, barely distinguishable in the dimness, and beckoned. Quietly they retraced their steps to the door, moved out onto the landing, and returned to the horses. The street still lay deserted and in shadows, but here and there lamplight glowed in a window. It would not be long before Larned was awake and prudence dictated they be well on their way by that moment.

Still leading the horses with the thought in mind to keep the sound of their passage at a minimum, Mungor and Sonny hurried to the jail — a low, flat-roofed structure of timbers stacked flat and solidly secured to form a square dungeon. The front wall presented but one window, no more than six inches in height and twenty-four in length, placed not far from the door. Halting at the side of the grim-looking affair where the horses would not be visible to the town, Sonny leaned close to the narrow grating.

"Larch! It's us — me and Mungor. We've come to bust you out."

"Where the hell you been?" Larch's muffled response was immediate, angry. "Been waiting all night."

Mungor had stepped to the door, was wedging the tip of the bar under the padlock in the hasp. At the third application of his weight, the lock broke and the iron crossbar dropped to the ground. Tossing the pry aside, Mungor pulled the door open. Larch, empty whiskey bottle in his hand, lunged into the open as if unable to stay inside the structure one second longer.

He drew up in front of the two men, a squat, threatening shape in the growing light. "Ain't got no answer to what I was asking yet! Where you been all night?"

Sonny looked away. Mungor returned the gunman's stare coolly. "I figured locked up in there was the best place for you — shape you were in."

Larch seemed to crouch lower. "You telling me you just left me in there — sweating it out in that stinking, black hole?"

"Was scared you'd get into more trouble, something bad that'd —"

Furious, Larch rocked forward. His fist shot out. Mungor, expecting just such a reaction, tried to sidestep, was too slow. The gunman's blow caught him on the jaw, sent him to his knees.

"Damn you!" Larch grated, surging in. "I'll kill you for —"

"Back off, Larch!" Sonny's voice sliced through the sudden tension. "We done it for you — for your own good, just like Mungor says."

Larch hesitated, his dark, bewhiskered features strained. The whites of his eyes

141

shone starkly in the gloom as he looked past the younger man at Mungor, face livid, gun in hand, and rising swiftly to his feet.

"Back off — both of you!" Sonny yelled, repeating himself.

Both Larch and Mungor hesitated. The gunman swore deeply. "My own good — like hell!" he said in a raspy voice. "They threw me in there once — for a whole month! You know what it's like cooped up in a stinking hole —"

"No, and I don't give a damn," Mungor cut in, his manner now easing as he slid his weapon back into its holster. Turning, he glanced over his shoulder toward the center of town. Two men, vague shapes in the early light, were moving in their direction. He came back around to Larch. "If you're of a mind to carry this on a bit farther, I'll accommodate you — but it'll have to be later. Time we got out of here."

"We done robbed that store," Sonny explained.

The gunman's coiled figure relented slightly. "You already cleaned it out?"

"Sure did," Sonny said, starting toward the horses. "Mungor sized it up last night. Was easy — like shooting fish in a rain barrel."

Mungor had pivoted, was also moving off

to his mount. Larch stood motionless for a few moments and, then wheeling, hurled the empty whiskey bottle through the open doorway of the jail. At the sound of glass shattering against the inner wall, he spun, stalked rigidly to his horse. Pausing there, he strapped on his gun and then swung up into the saddle.

"This ain't over yet, mister!" he snarled, glaring at Mungor.

"It was as much me as him!" Sonny declared, his voice rising. "Don't go faulting him for all of it!"

"You ain't got no better sense," Larch said in a cold voice. "He does; he knows what it's like to be locked up and the key throwed away."

Mungor shook his head, spat. "We're getting mighty sick and tired of you bleating like a goat about getting locked up," he said, taking up the reins. "I doubt if there's a man alive who ain't got something that chews on him — but he usually keeps it to himself. That's something you ought to do. . . . Now, let's get out of here before we all wind up inside that jail."

"Where we headed?" Sonny asked quickly, anxious to bring an end to the harsh, heated words being exchanged. "What's the next place on your list?"

"Hays City," Mungor replied, as they moved off. "Not far from here — and the bank there looks after the payroll for the army at Fort Hays."

Deputy Ben Houston, astride his bay gelding, the little buckskin pack horse trailing quietly at the end of a short rope, was a solitary silhouette as he moved patiently across the ridge he was following.

Somewhere in the broad country ahead were the three killers he had been sent to track down — and on their shoulders rode his future; if he found them and brought them down one way or another, it was assured — if he failed, it was at an end.

But it was a big land, and they could be anywhere. Abilene — that was the last trace he had of them. They could still be in that area and, for all he knew, they could now be in Texas, or Nebraska, or Colorado — any of a dozen other places, in fact.

But it was what he expected. Smart outlaws kept on the move, were never fools enough to tarry long in one vicinity. Sooner or later, however, they made a mistake, and it was his job to be there when this bunch committed theirs — or at least close by. And he would be. Eventually a pattern would form, take shape, and he could start think-

144

ing as they did. Then it would be simple to figure ahead and, somewhere, be waiting.

Houston drew the bay to a halt. Reaching down, he shifted the holstered pistol on his thigh a bit forward. Two riders had appeared on the trail, coming into view as they broke out of a band of brush, and approached him. Pulling off his hat, the deputy ran his fingers through the shock of sandy hair covering his head, wiped at the sweat on his brow with the back of a hand, and studied the oncoming riders with calculating interest. . . . Two cowpunchers, he guessed. Probably drifting west to greener pastures.

"Howdy," he greeted as they halted in front of him. "Hot day."

"Sure is," the older of the pair agreed. Both wore range clothing, a bit ragged, but the younger man was sporting a new pair of boots.

"Where you headed?" he asked.

Houston smiled faintly at the brash question, but he was looking for information too and let it pass. "Abilene way. Aim to look up some friends. You from around there?"

"No, we're coming from Wichita," the older cowhand replied.

"Town's in a hullabaloo," his partner continued. "Bank was robbed by some of the James gang."

Houston frowned. "That so? Heard they was on the loose again. Anybody get hurt?"

"Nope, reckon not. Just walked in, helped themselves to the money in the safe — same as they done at Abilene — and at Emporia, too, we heard."

Emporia . . . Houston hadn't heard about the gang going there, just as the robbery at Wichita was also news. "How much money'd they get at Wichita?"

"Around six thousand dollars," the younger man said. "Sure sounds like a easy way to make a living."

Houston rubbed at the stubble on his chin, shook his head. "Well, it ain't," he said. "Good talking to you." Nodding to the men, he moved on.

Abilene — Emporia — Wichita. Where in Kansas would the killers strike next? It was still too early to foresee; but one thing was certain — they were following a plan, one that entailed a string of continuing robberies that would enable them to steadily accumulate money. They were unlike the usual, run-of-the-mill outlaws, who robbed, took what loot they had garnered, and then drew off somewhere to spend and enjoy it; this bunch had higher stakes in mind, probably aiming for a fortune. When a certain goal was reached, they'd divide and go separate ways, disappearing either across the Canadian border or on south into Mexico.

He reckoned he'd best forget Abilene now and make tracks for Wichita, see what he could learn there. One thing was definite, and helpful: they were confining their activities to Kansas — and, just possibly, were beginning to work south if you figured they had started from Abilene, which was a bit of good luck for him if true.

This job just might end sooner than expected, but he'd not go counting chickens just yet — not until they hatched. Ben Houston had learned the fallacy of that many years ago.

16

They rode boldly down the center of Hays City's main street — three men wearing wide-brimmed hats and tan-colored dusters — and drew no unwarranted attention. The settlement lay on the main road to Denver and other points in the Rockies. Strangers were not unusual, and the majority of Kansas men wore the long coats as protection from dust as well as the sun and hot winds.

"There's the bank," Mungor said, not pointing at a small, solid-looking building standing on a corner but indicating it with a slight nod. "Little early yet. Need to kill time until near closing."

"As soon we'd pull up somewheres and stop," Sonny said, shifting in his saddle. "Sure am mighty tired of setting."

Larch had no comment then, just as he had remained sullen and silent during the entire trip from Larned. Mungor had ignored it, knowing the incident at the jail was still festering in the gunman's mind, but he was determined it should not interfere with his plans, now riding the heady crest of success. They would take the Hays City bank — which should be good for at least ten thousand — and then head due south, perhaps find another fat little store on the way, and clean it out just for the hell of it.

"We're running low on grub," Sonny said as they continued on. "Water, too. You reckon we ought to do some stocking up here?"

"I'm heading for that saloon," Larch said, finally finding his voice. Abruptly cutting away from his partners, he angled toward a small bar a short distance off the street.

A hard, tight smile pulled at Mungor's lips as he watched the man go. After a bit he turned to Sonny. "Stay with him — he's out of whiskey. Maybe after he gets himself a fresh bottle, he'll be in a better mind. I'll buy a little grub and meet you and him there when it's time to pay a call on the bank."

Sonny bobbed happily, the prospects of finding female companionship with which to while away a few hours suddenly dawning upon him.

"Want you to see to your own canteen — Larch's too," Mungor said, and rode on, pausing to add over a shoulder: "Best you forget the women. Won't be time enough."

Sonny grinned broadly, spurred away. "Don't worry none about me," he said as he hurried to overtake Larch.

Mungor continued along the street until he located a store. There he purchased the items necessary to replenish their dwindling trail grub and refilled his canteen with water from a pitcher pump at the side of the building. That done, under the watchful eyes of the storekeeper, a slight, bespectacled man who reeked of suspicion, he rode on, ostensibly heading north out of town. When he was well out of the man's sight, Mungor cut left and, taking the long way around, circled back to the saloon.

It was still an hour or so to the time when he deemed best for robbing the bank, and pulling in beside Sonny and Larch's horses, he dismounted and tied up next to them. Hanging his saddlebags over a shoulder — they now contained nothing but money since he'd transferred his cooking gear to the grub sack — he entered the low-roofed building and glanced around. The place was deserted except for the bartender and Larch sitting at a table in a far corner, bottle before him. Sonny was not to be seen.

"Near to catching up on your boozing?" Mungor asked caustically, crossing the room and sitting down opposite the gunman.

Larch raised his brooding eyes to him. "It bother'n you some?"

"Not a damn bit," the tall man replied, taking a swallow of whiskey direct from the bottle.

"You got any bellyaching to do about me not holding up my end of the deal?"

"Not specially —"

"Then I ain't expecting to hear you bad-mouthing me about it again," Larch said, refilling his own glass. "When we hitting this here bank you claim's full of money?"

"Can start pretty quick," Mungor said, glancing at the sky through the dust- and smoke-filmed window behind the gunman. Evidently Larch was allowing his ire over the incident at Larned to cool, finally, and meant to carry it no farther. "They'll be getting ready to close up in a few more minutes."

Mungor swung his attention to a door in the back of the saloon. It had opened suddenly to admit Sonny, his arm around a slovenly, dark girl with stringy, ill-kept hair and wearing a torn, red dress.

"Looks like the kid's ready," Larch said

151

dryly. The gunman could have also added that his supply of liquor — in addition to the half-empty bottle on the table before him, another full quart was visible in his coat pocket — had been replenished and he, too, was ready, but he did not.

Mungor nodded, beckoned to Sonny, and, rising, started for the door. Larch followed and, after a minute or two spent with the girl, Sonny joined them.

"Time to go to work?" he asked jovially.

Mungor said, "Just about. We'll ride up to the hitch rack, like we was coming to do business. Plan's the same once we get inside — you watch the door; Larch, you keep an eye on the folks while I empty the safe."

"I been wanting to do a mite of talking about that," the gunman said, crossing to his horse and jerking the lines free. "Soon as we get done here, I'll be wanting my share — all of it. Reckon I'm old enough to look after my own money."

Mungor gave that thought, seeing in it, perhaps, the first signs of the partnership breaking up. "Fine with me. Next stop we make after we get out of here, you'll get it," he said as he mounted. He turned then to Sonny. "You feel the same way?"

The younger man, already in the saddle, shrugged. "Makes no never-mind to me. I'd rather you'd look after it for me, but if you want to get shed of it, I'll take mine, too — long as we ain't splitting up."

"That what you're figuring on, Larch?" Mungor put the question bluntly to the gunman.

"Nope, ain't nothing changed far as I'm concerned," he said. "We just keep right on going. It's only that I feel better toting my own poke."

It would be something of a relief to hand over the part of the money that wasn't his, Mungor decided. Not only would he be ridding himself of the responsibility for it, but the sacks had become heavy and difficult to carry.

Pulling about, Mungor cut away from the rack into the center of the street, with Sonny on his left, Larch to the right. Shadows were beginning to lengthen and stretch away from the buildings and the pulse of the settlement had slowed even more.

He could see two men leaning against the wall of a building a short distance down the way as they conversed, and a lone woman strolled indolently along a sidewalk as she went about her late afternoon marketing. Dogs were barking somewhere beyond the town, and from a church, not visible because of intervening commercial structures, came the mournful sound of a bell tolling.

Reaching the intersecting street, Mungor threw his glance to the bank. The door was still open. They would arrive there at about the exact, preferred time.

"No gunplay," Mungor warned quietly as they turned the corner and pointed for the building. "Army post is close by and we sure don't want them —"

At that moment half a dozen cavalrymen, being led by a young spit-and-polish second lieutenant, wheeled into view just beyond the bank. The patrol slowed as the officer, surprise blanking his features, raised a gloved hand.

"It's them!" one of the soldiers yelled suddenly. "It's that holdup gang acoming to rob this here bank, I'll bet!"

Mungor delayed no longer. They had ridden into the equivalent of a trap, one that had not been awaiting them, to be sure, but equally deadly. Jamming spurs into the flanks of his horse, he spun the animal around, headed back down the narrow street along which they had come. He heard Sonny yell, then the blast of Larch's pistol came to him, but he did not look back to see if one of the soldiers had been hit or if the gunman had fired in hopes of delaying them; the important thing was to gain the building — a stable it appeared to be — and round it before the soldiers could open up on them.

They reached it just as the cavalrymen brought their weapons into play. Bullets thudded into the wall of the livery barn, kicked up dust about the horses' hoofs; one caromed off Mungor's saddle horn. He risked a side glance at his two companions as they veered sharply around the end of the stable. Both had their pistols out, and as they raced in behind the bulking structure, they leveled and fired at the patrol, now without its young commanding officer and coming at them at full gallop.

Mungor threw a hurried look ahead. They could not hope for the cover of darkness to aid them, at least not yet; it was still an hour or more away. And their horses were not in the best condition, having had only sporadic bits of rest along the road from Larned. A continuing race with the cavalrymen could only end in the patrol's favor.

A narrow lane flanked by tall cane appeared to his left. Unhesitating, Mungor swerved into it, hearing the hammer of Larch and Sonny's horses immediately behind him. The exchange of shots between his partners and the soldiers was now a steady racket, and the patrol seemed no closer. So far he and his partners were being able to maintain a small lead — but it wouldn't last for long, he realized grimly.

The lane ended at a small farm house. As they raced into its yard, a man and a woman, with several small children, attracted by the sound of the running horses, had come into the open to see what was happening. All crowded back against the front of the soddy as Mungor, with Sonny and Larch snapping bullets at the pursuing soldiers, thundered past them and galloped for a small island of trees and brush a short distance beyond.

At that point Mungor drew his weapon and, bent low, began to add his shots to those of his partners. If they could slow the cavalrymen long enough to reach the brush, they'd have a fair chance of shaking them.

They gained the welter of sunflowers, doveweed, oak, and other scraggly growth, interspersed here and there with stunted trees. Once well into it and beyond sight of the soldiers, Mungor cut hard right to break the straight line of their flight, began to swing wide and double back into the same direction they had just come.

A dozen yards and they pulled up short in a shallow ravine, horses heaving and plastered with foam, their own bodies soaking in sweat. A dozen yards away the patrol, weapons now silent since the enemy was no longer visible, rushed by — the crashing sounds of their passage all too close.

When they were safely gone, Mungor turned to Larch and Sonny. The gunman was quietly reloading his pistol, his stolid, dark features set. He seemingly was unaware of the blood streak across the back of a hand where a bullet had left its track. Sonny, nearby, was smiling, his eyes filled with the excitement of the past minutes.

"Things sure didn't work out so good, did they?" he commented, mopping at his forehead.

Mungor's shoulders stirred. "No way of knowing that bunch of yellowlegs'd show up —"

"Should've figured on it," Larch cut in dourly. "That there fort's right close by."

Sonny's face sobered as he recognized the signs of trouble between the two men again. "Was worth trying for, anyway," he said quickly, "but we sure better get the hell out of here fast! Them boys ain't going to quit looking for us — not after we dropped that lieutenant —"

"Was me that done that," Larch said. "Don't go taking on my blame. I figured it was the only way we could slow them down long enough to get away."

Mungor said nothing, his first failure leaving a bitter taste in his mouth — but shooting the officer had probably saved their lives, he had to admit. However, it was no time to dawdle; as Sonny had noted they had best move out quickly.

"Let's get out of here," he said.

"Where'll we head for?" Sonny asked. "Them soldier boys'll be combing Kansas like a —"

"South, for the Indian Territory," Mungor cut in. "Strip down there called No Man's Land where the law, or the soldiers, can't come. We can lay low for a few days till things blow over."

17

They moved off through the brush with care, walking the horses slowly, endeavoring to create as little noise as possible since there was no way of knowing where the soldiers were. The members of the patrol could have separated, Mungor feared, and each could be searching through the dense growth, now filling with deep shadows as darkness closed in steadily.

But by the time night with its concealing cloak had fallen completely, Mungor, trailed in Indian fashion by Larch and Sonny, had broken clear of the heavy scrub and was bearing southwest for the lower corner of the state.

"We stopping over at Buffalo City?" Sonny asked near midnight when they halted in a small grove to rest the horses as well as themselves. There was a note of hope in the younger man's voice as he entertained thoughts of his female acquaintances at the

Palace Saloon.

"Don't you never think of nothing but women?" Larch demanded sourly, stretching out on the cool stub grass.

Sonny laughed. In the pale moonlight showering down from a velvet sky, he looked even younger than he was.

"Sure can't remember nothing better to do in my spare time — and it sure beats sucking on a bottle of whiskey. . . . What about it, Mungor?"

The tall man had taken the last of the stogies he'd bought in Larned from a pocket, was examining it thoughtfully. It had broken, and after a moment he tossed it aside.

"Be pushing our luck," he said. "Those soldiers won't give up on us, so we best get across the line fast as we can." He paused briefly, added with a faint smile: "We've done a pretty fair job of cleaning out Kansas, anyways."

"For a fact," Sonny murmured. "Expect them badge-toters are going plumb looney trying to find us. . . . You want me to build a fire so's we can boil up some coffee?"

"Nope, better pass it up. Fire can be seen for plenty of miles across them flats. Best we wait for morning."

But with the first streaks of light in the east, Mungor, plagued by a feeling of

160

uneasiness, elected to move on without taking the time necessary to prepare a meal. Larch and Sonny, having by then learned through experience to respect the man's judgment, made no complaint.

They rode steadily but did not press their horses while Mungor, not relying on his two partners who dozed in the saddle most of the time, maintained a continual watch on their back trail. Twice he saw riders, but the distance was too great to tell if they were soldiers or not. He refused to gamble on it and each time veered off into lower ground where they would not be silhouetted and draw the attention of the horsemen.

They were a long three days and a considerable part of several nights reaching the outlaw sanctuary known as No Man's Land; but it was only when they had come to a deserted shack familiar to Mungor, and which he knew definitely was well within the lawless panhandle, that he breathed easier.

They were all bone-tired from the continuing ride, had eaten but little; and after settling in the shack, taking care of the horses, and bolting a hastily prepared meal, they stretched out on their blankets and slept the sleep of the near exhausted which extended almost around the clock.

"How long we camping here?" Larch wanted to know, morosely considering his near-empty whiskey bottle.

It was the following morning and all three men were hunched around a fire over which a pan of chunked sow-belly and sliced potatoes was sizzling noisily. Nearby, coffee was rumbling quietly in the pot as it began to boil.

"Day or two," Mungor replied, stirring the contents of the spider with his skinning knife. "Won't hurt the horses none to rest up a bit — it's a long way yet to the Mex border."

Larch nodded. "Yeh," he agreed, and then faced the tall men accusingly. "Seems I recollect you was going to do something a time back — before we headed south. Kid, pass him them saddlebags of his'n. Now's as good a place as any to divvy up that cash."

Sonny threw a questioning glance at Mungor. The tall man merely shrugged, indicating it was neither here nor there with him. Rising, the younger man picked up the leather pouches lying close by and dropped them at Mungor's feet. Sheathing his knife, he unbuckled the bags and parceled out their shares, dividing the gold equally with the currency.

"Figures up to about twelve thousand apiece," he said.

Sonny, as if struck dumb, was fondling the packs of bills, the smooth, gold coins in a dazed sort of way. After a bit he swallowed noisily.

"Lord — Lord!" he muttered in a breathless voice.

Mungor's lips cracked into a tight smile. "We ought to double that by the time we reach El Paso — if our luck'll hold out."

"It'll hold out," the younger man declared confidently, still fondling the eagles. "Mostly, 'cause you're our good luck, and long as we're running together it will. Ain't that so, Larch?"

The gunman made no reply. He had taken an old shirt from his saddlebags, ripped it into a long strip and, placing his money on it, was folding it into a sort of belt which he evidently intended to wear around his waist out of sight.

"Reckon so," he said finally in a grudging tone as he thrust his gold eagles into a pocket.

Mungor smiled again as he returned his portion of the cash to one of the canvas sacks and restored it to his leather bags, now considerably lighter and lacking any bulge. Larch found it hard to admit matters had gone well despite the setback at Hays City, was finding it even more difficult to attribute their success to the leadership and planning of someone other than himself. It didn't matter to Mungor; he was profiting as much financially as were Larch and Sonny, and that was all that counted. Little by little he was drawing nearer to his goal of the good life in Mexico.

"Well, if it ain't the James boys —"

At the words Mungor froze, and then turned slowly. Four men, pistols in their hands, were standing behind them. They had approached from the opposite side of the shack, and although Larch had been facing that direction, he had been so engrossed in improvising a means for carrying his money that their presence had gone unnoticed.

Sonny, his features suddenly taut, had come upright, hand dropping toward the weapon on his hip. One of the men, a thick-bodied, black-bearded rider with a brass-studded hat band on a narrow-brimmed hat, shook his head warningly.

"You that anxious to die, boy? I'd purely hate to blow your guts all over the place."

Mungor, making his movements deliberate and without threat, came to his feet. "Grub ain't much but you're welcome — if

164

that's what you're looking for," he said, sizing up the party.

All were trail-worn, lean-faced hardcases hiding from the law in the strip, just as were they.

"Eating ain't what we're here for, is it, boys?" the heavy-set man said with a short laugh. "We been hearing all about you three jaspers and how you been cleaning out banks all over Kansas, and when we spotted you riding in, we had a hunch you was the ones. Know it for a fact now."

An older member of the party pushed forward and looked closely at Mungor and his partners. After a bit he stepped back.

"You ain't none of the James bunch," he stated flatly. "Leastwise you ain't none of them I've ever seen."

"Never claimed to be," Mungor said, sliding a glance at Larch.

The gunman was hunched on his heels, arms loose at his sides while his dead-level eyes drilled unblinkingly into the outlaws. Although there was no prearranged plan should a situation such as this ever arise, Mungor knew he had only to give the slightest signal and Larch would spring into deadly action. Just as there were certain unwritten laws, so also there was an understood code existing between men of their calling during such taut moments.

The black-bearded man gestured with his pistol at the saddlebags at Mungor's feet. "How about you kicking them bags over here to me, mister — and then old ugly there with that whiskey bottle can toss me that ragful of money he's so proud of. Be wanting what you got there, too, kid — and don't none of you start thinking about going for your iron. They's four of us to your three and we're right jumpy."

Mungor lowered his head, again threw another glance at the gunman — this time one filled with intent.

Larch stirred slightly. "Well, might as well have mine now," he drawled, and reached for the bulky strip of cloth stretched out before him on the ground. "But first off I reckon —"

The remainder of his words were lost in the sudden, shocking blast of his pistol. Mungor, spinning, drew fast, fired also. The outlaws rocked backward. The heavy-set one dropped like a stone as bullets slammed into him. The tall, older man yelled in pain, staggered, fell. Mungor felt the heat of a lead slug skimming his cheek, another his arm, and swore. They had been close, but as during the war, he was untouched. The charm still held.

Slowly he straightened up, pistol ready as smoke and dust floated about him and his two partners. The only sound now was the burbling of the coffee and the crackling of the frying meat and potatoes, left too long on the fire and turning dark and hard.

The four outlaws lay in various positions on the weedy ground, no longer involved in life and therefore with no interest in gold. Larch, stoically reloading his pistol, was paying no attention to them. Sonny, his weapon out and also being replenished, was staring at the dead men, a curious disdain on his young features.

Putting his attention then to his own six gun, Mungor replaced the spent cartridges and thrust the weapon into its holster. Pivoting, he squatted and removed the spider from the fire.

"Let's eat — get out of here," he said, portioning out the food. "Shots'll be bringing us more visitors."

"So they come!" Sonny said, his voice high and tight with excitement. "Expect we've done proved we can look out for ourselves!"

"No doubt," Mungor admitted, "but we'd be fools to ask for trouble. The country around here is crawling with the likes of them. Next time it might be a dozen instead of only four."

Larch had leathered his weapon, wrapped the money belt about his middle, and was beginning to eat.

"Ain't nothing ever changes," he said in his dour way. "Getting something's only half of the game. Keeping it's the rest. . . . Where we going from here?"

"Las Vegas — over in New Mexico," Mungor answered. "Couple of big gambling houses there that ought to do real good by us."

"Who the blue hell are you, anyway?" the gray-whiskered old sergeant demanded in a peevish voice as he swiped at his dust-rimmed mouth with a freckled hand.

"Name's Ben Houston — deputy sheriff," the lawman said, producing his star. "Ain't questioning your word, but are you pretty sure these are the same three outlaws that've been doing all the bank robbing and killing across the state?"

The noncom swore loudly. He and the patrol had been out searching the plains day and night since the moment when Lieutenant Hutchins had been shot out of his saddle, and he was in no mood for a lot of useless talk.

"Of course I'm sure, damn it! Tall fellow, a skinny kid, and a bull-neck — the one that shot the lieutenant. Ain't likely to forget, or make a mistake."

"I reckon you won't. Just that I have to be sure the ones you've been chasing and that lit out for the panhandle are the same ones."

"Saying it once more — and not again! We've been on their trail ever since Hays City. Run them into the brakes, lost them. Picked up their trail later about halfway to Buffalo City, then lost it again. But they was ahead of us, I know that, same as I know they was legging it for No Man's Land."

"Would make sense," Houston said, more to himself than the noncom.

From the ranks of the weary soldiers a voice said: "Sarge, can't we head back to the Fort now?"

Houston glanced at the elderly man, "Guess you ain't got a choice —"

The sergeant nodded wearily. "Sure ain't. We can't cross over into that damned nest of rattlesnakes, though I'd give a year's pay to go in there — alone — after them. The lieutenant was a friend of mine. How long've you been tracking them, Deputy?"

Houston pulled off his hat, scratched at his head. "Ever since they held up a bank in Denver and done some killing. Been quite a spell, seems."

"Expect you know you ain't got no authority to go in there either."

The lawman smiled, shook his head. "Been out of where I got any authority ever since I crossed my county line, back in Colorado, but I ain't letting that stop me. Was put on the job and told to bring them in — or cut them down. I aim to do one or the other."

The noncom considered that for several moments, and then wagged his head wearily. "Sure wish't I could swap places with you, but I reckon there ain't much chance of that. . . . Good luck."

"Obliged, and same to you," Houston said as the sergeant raised his hand and, croaking a command, started his men back up the trail they had just traveled.

Good luck. . . . The words lodged in Deputy Ben Houston's mind, hung there. He'd need luck, and plenty of it — but he reckoned he hadn't done so badly. So far fortune had treated him pretty well, in fact.

He'd been spared a vast amount of chasing back and forth across Kansas, having by mere chance encountered first two pilgrims who had passed along information that helped him locate the killers — or at least the general area where they had last been seen, and then encountering days later a

170

patrol from Fort Hays that was also on their trail.

Running into the soldiers was the best break of all; they had actually met, shot it out with, and then pursued the killers and sent them scurrying for the safety of No Man's Land. All in all he had probably been saved weeks of riding.

What would they do next? Where would they most likely go after a few days of laying around in the panhandle? There was nothing left for them in Kansas now — and they certainly wouldn't risk going back to Cheyenne or Denver. Las Vegas, over in adjoining New Mexico Territory — odds were they'd head for there! Not only did the settlement boast of a fair-sized bank, but there were also several big gambling houses. Houston reckoned he'd be smart to do a bit of gambling himself — on his hunch — and line out for the settlement right fast.

18

Mungor halted in a grove of stubby piñon trees at the edge of the lush, broad grassland in which Las Vegas lay. Towering beyond the settlement were the peaks of the rugged mountain range that early-arriving Spaniards, laboring across the endless land in clanking armor, had named the Sangre de Cristos.

"Don't look like much," Larch said, taking a swig from his bottle and returning it to the side pocket of his duster without offering it to either Mungor or Sonny — as was his usual way.

"Looks don't always count for much," Mungor countered in a dry voice.

"You been here before?" Sonny asked, hooking a leg over the saddle horn to ease his muscles.

"Yeh, four, maybe five months ago. Looked the place over same as I have the others. Couple of saloons and gambling houses on the east side of town. Can forget about the bank and the rest of it. Was told folks come here for their health, try to get over being sick."

"That's what we're coming for — to get well," Sonny said with a laugh. "Only the kind of medicine we're after is money. We doing it same as always — splitting up and riding in alone?"

"Same as before," Mungor said. "You come in from the south, Larch from the west side. I'll ride in from here. Don't forget — we don't know each other and —"

"What's wrong with me going in from the main road instead of you?" Larch demanded, rubbing at his stubble-covered jaw. "How about you doing the circling around to the yonder side?"

"Makes no difference to me," Mungor said, resignedly. "But if you do, take off that duster and clean yourself up a mite. You've got outlaw written all over you, and the town badge'll stop you before you get —"

"All right, all right," Larch cut in angrily. "I'll do the circling around. Where we meeting up?" The gunman had begun to remove his long coat preparatory to stowing it inside his saddlebags.

"Biggest casino's in the Bonanza Saloon. It'll be the one we'll clean out — probably around midnight since that's when the crowd starts thinning out. Could be later, or it could be earlier. Can get rooms there — and there's a stable out back."

"Sure wouldn't fret me none was we to hold off and hang around a couple of days," Sonny said, again shifting his position. "I've dang nigh growed to this saddle."

Larch grunted and took a drink from his bottle, now being carried inside his partly unbuttoned shirt.

"You sure it ain't because it's been a spell since you had some gal?"

Sonny grinned. "Well, now, that just could be it," he said. "I purely can't recollect —"

"You both got it straight?" Mungor cut in impatiently. "It's the Bonanza we're putting up in, so I don't want you doing anything to mess us up. Place could be good for four, maybe five thousand dollars."

Larch considered the town skeptically. Somewhere in the distance meadowlarks were whistling cheerily. "Why'd there be so much money in a two-bit burg like this'n?"

"Folks are expecting the railroad to come, same as they were in Buffalo City. Some of them are getting ready."

Larch spat. "Hell — it could be years —"

"Maybe it will and maybe it won't — point is, saloons are springing up all along the right of way so's they'll be there ready and waiting. The Bonanza and the others in Las Vegas are doing real good anyway. There's a lot of traveling on the Santa Fe Trail, and since most wagons are taking the cutoff, they come straight into the town."

The gunman secured the cork in his bottle of whiskey with a slap of his palm and tucked it back inside his shirt.

"Well, whatever you're saying, I reckon me and Sonny'll swallow," he said, fingering closed the buttons.

Mungor lifted his reins, studying the squat man blandly. "I've made the offer before, Larch, and I'm making it again now — pull out whenever you've got the notion. Means nothing to me one way or the other."

The gunman laughed, a small, unfamiliar, strained sound. "Oh, I'm hanging around, bucko!" he said. "I wasn't standing behind the door when good sense was being passed out! With you running this outfit, getting rich is mighty easy."

Mungor made no response, simply watched the man pull away and head due west through the thick trees to disappear from view in only moments.

"Expect I'd best be riding, too," Sonny said, settling back into his saddle. "Be seeing you later."

■ ■ ■ ■

It was one hell of a place, Sonny decided, as he stood on the balcony of the Bonanza's second floor and looked down upon the activity surging back and forth below in a confusion of sound, smoke, and smells.

As usual Mungor had been right. The saloon teemed with customers drawn from everywhere, he guessed, and money flowed like water. Sonny reckoned if he was any judge, he and his partners would be taking double the amount of cash Mungor had estimated when they robbed the casino.

The tall man had yet to show, which was to be expected. Mungor would see first to his horse; then, since it was early, he'd seek out a barbershop, treat himself to a bath, shave, and probably a haircut.

That's where Sonny had it all over the man. He didn't worry too much about things like that, ordinarily performing such chores quickly in his quarters so that he might be free to seek out female companionship as soon as possible.

He had already rented a room, cleaned up, enjoyed the company of a well-turned little Mexican señorita who called herself Juana, partaken of a most satisfying meal in the restaurant adjacent to the Bonanza, and was now ready for further diversion.

He didn't take much to gambling. He was a poor loser, and losing money was his idea of damn foolishness. There were better and more satisfying ways of getting rid of it.

He supposed he could go down, take a stroll along the street, have a look into some of the other saloons strung out along its length, but that had no strong appeal either. The Bonanza was by far the largest and enjoyed the most trade, and —

"You look lonesome, cowboy."

Sonny pivoted. A smile parted his lips. It was a woman he had noticed earlier in the restaurant, sitting alone at a back table. Dark-haired, dark-eyed, with the perfectly shaped face of a doll, she was dressed all in white, with much lace and other frills in evidence. Unquestionably, she was the most beautiful woman he'd ever seen!

"Seeing something like you sure can make a fellow lonesome," he said. "Folks I like call me Sonny."

The woman, evidently having come from one of the rooms down the hallway, moved nearer. The smell of her perfume sent blood pounding in his temples.

"I'm Dolly," she said. "That painting on the wall downstairs — you might have noticed it — is of me. . . . Weren't you in the restaurant a while ago?"

Sonny made no response. Recalling the portrait of the reclining nude suspended above the saloon's backbar had sent his pulses thundering even faster. Women such as pictured he had always believed were only in the painter's imagination; but here was this one — a beauty that fairly robbed a man of his breath — in the flesh!

"Yeh — I seen you, too," he said, finally in answer to her question. "Was trying to catch your eye, get you to speak."

Dolly merely smiled, dabbed at her faintly rouged cheeks with a pale blue handkerchief.

"You work here?" Sonny asked hopefully. He was reveling in the thought of spending time with the sort of woman who he believed existed only in dreams.

"Yes," Dolly said, "but I'm not just one of the girls. I'm real particular — and I'm expensive. But I'm worth it."

"I'll just bet my best pair of spurs you are," Sonny said admiringly as the woman, arms akimbo, pivoted slowly to display her figure. "How about me and you getting us a bottle and spending some time in my room?"

Dolly shrugged, her smooth, round shoulders stirring gently under the silky fabric of her dress. "No reason why we can't — long as you've got enough money."

Sonny swore quietly. Never had he hoped to find, much less possess, a woman such as Dolly. "Money ain't nothing to me," he said, grandly. "I got more'n plenty."

Dolly smiled wryly. "I've heard that tune before, but when it came to counting out the cash —"

Sonny patted the bulge that encircled his middle. He had taken his cue from Larch, fashioning himself a money belt from a strip of cloth.

"It's here — right here," he said, and then thrusting a hand into a side pocket, he clinked several gold eagles together. "Got more there. What do you say now?"

"I'm ready," Dolly murmured, slipping her arm under his and starting to turn. Abruptly, she came to a halt. "Oh, my God!" she added in a stricken voice.

Sonny, off balance from her sudden stop, glanced at her in wonder and surprise. Dolly's eyes, spread wide and filled with fear, were fixed on the doorway of the saloon. Anger rising within him at the interruption, Sonny swung his attention to that point. A frown drew his brow into deep furrows. Mungor had just entered, was standing there glancing about.

"A hundred saloons in this country — maybe a thousand — and he has to walk into this one," she said in a low, exhausted voice.

"Him — that tall man?" Sonny said, coming back to her. "You know him?"

Dolly nodded slowly. "Was my husband — once. I left him during the war — ran off with another man. He'll kill me when he sees me."

Mungor's wife . . . Sonny recalled what Larch had repeated to him the time the tall man had thawed slightly and revealed a time in his past. Mungor hadn't stretched the truth about one thing — she was the most beautiful woman he'd ever seen.

"Your name's Darsie —"

The woman, startled, stared at him. "You — you know him — and about me?"

Sonny nodded. "He's a friend of mine. How does it happen you didn't see him when he was here a few months ago?"

"I wasn't around, I guess. Only been here a short while." Dolly shrugged. "Well, I guess it all ends here."

Sonny shook his head. "Don't worry none about me telling him. We ain't that good of friends."

"It won't matter," she said, helplessly.

180

"Nothing will now. He'll see that painting over the bar, recognize me, and start asking questions. The bartender will tell him I'm here — upstairs, room Ten. That's all he'll need."

Sonny was seeing his night in paradise slipping away — all because of his partner, but he couldn't find it in himself to let Mungor harm Dolly regardless of what had happened in the past. Visualizing her crumpled on the floor, brutally beaten — dead, brought a hardness to his eyes. It would never take place — not if he could help it! Even if he was to get all of the cash they expected to make from the Bonanza for his share — it still wouldn't be worth it.

"Don't you fret," he said in a low, determined voice, as he took her by the shoulders and started her back down the hall. "I'll take care of Mungor. You just keep out of sight for a bit."

19

"Sure is one hell of a note!" Larch grumbled as they rode quickly off into the warm afternoon. "We could've laid our hands on ten, maybe fifteen thousand dollars!"

They were heading south out of the town, sticking close to the trees and brush that grew thick along the creek running through the settlement.

Mungor had scarcely spoken since their hasty departure but now, hunched forward on his horse, reins gripped in his left hand, the right resting on his thigh, he swore deeply and shook his head.

"You're right, Larch. We could've made a cleaning there — likely the biggest we'll ever see." He hesitated, staring straight ahead. In the softening light the tall man's rugged features appeared to be of bronze. Abruptly he turned his attention to Sonny, riding nearby. "Who was this jasper that tipped you off about them laying for us?"

The younger man brushed at his mouth with the back of a hand. In the stream just beyond him a trout plopped noisily as it came out of the cold water for an insect.

"Didn't say I got tipped off about it," he corrected. "Said I heard some fellows talking — vigilantes, I reckon they were."

"How the hell'd they know we'd be there? That's something I'd sure give a pile to know," Larch said, taking a swallow from his bottle.

"Mite interested in that myself," Mungor said. "You answer that, Sonny?"

"Nope, I can't! I've done told you all I could!"

"Which sure ain't much to lose all that cash over," Larch muttered.

"Damn it — it cost me, too!" Sonny declared, his voice rising angrily. "You both are acting like I ain't sorry we had to pass up robbing that place! Hell, I'm losing a third of what we would've got."

Mungor settled back in his saddle. There was no point in hashing over what was lost. They could do nothing about it now; the thing to do was look ahead to the next towns on his list — to the south, in the direction of the Mexican border. Five thousand, if that was what each might have had as his share of the Bonanza's casino cash, would have fattened their pokes considerably — but better nothing at all than being behind bars — or dead.

The question Larch had voiced minutes earlier came back to mind: How could the law, or the vigilantes, have known they were coming to Las Vegas? Was there someone on their trail, perhaps a lawman, with clever foresight, who was guessing at where they would next strike and getting the word there before they arrived? Troubled by that possibility, Mungor again turned to Sonny.

A look of wistfulness was on the younger man's face along with a sort of regretful smile. It was as if he were remembering something pleasant, something he treasured and was keeping locked in his memory. Mungor considered him for a long minute as they now loped steadily on, his eyes narrowing with suspicion; and then his shoulders stirred. Sonny wouldn't have queered their plans — not for any reason; money meant too much to him.

"Like to hear exactly what it was you heard them jaspers say —"

Sonny stared at him briefly, spat, swore raggedly. "Done told you once —"

"Want to hear it again — all of it."

"Why?" Sonny demanded, glancing at Larch as if for support. The gunman was dozing in the saddle, rocking gently to and fro with the motion of his horse. "Ain't nothing we can do about it now."

"Not saying there is, but it's got me to wondering if there's somebody on to us — a lawman or two, trying to set up a trap."

"Lawman?" Sonny echoed, frowning. "Hell, I don't see how."

"Those men you overheard talking said they was expecting a holdup — by three men, members of the James gang. That drops the loop over us. Now, what's got me to puzzling is how'd they know we were figuring to rob the Bonanza? In fact, how'd they even know we'd be in this part of the country? Last anybody seen of us we were up in Kansas."

Larch had not been asleep. He sat up abruptly, fortified himself with a drink from his bottle, and bobbed his head at Sonny.

"Them's mighty good questions! You wouldn't know the answer to them now, would you, boy?"

The younger man jerked his horse to a stop, anger and outrage stiffening his slight frame. "You trying to say I double-crossed you all?"

Larch, drawing up with Mungor, grinned in his cold, mirthless way. "I ain't trying to say nothing, boy. Mungor's talking sense —

something mighty rotten's going on and I ain't for sure —"

"Let it go," Mungor cut in. "I haven't tipped my plans to anybody — and I don't see how either one of you could have slipped up, because neither one of you knew where we were going until we were on the way.

"No, it wasn't none of us that let something slip. Word was here ahead of us for certain, and that's what's puzzling me. How'd it get here? Only answer to that is that somebody's got wise to us and's smart enough to figure out what we're doing."

"There ain't been nobody trailing us," Larch said, as they moved on. "I been watching."

Sonny, anger cooled, pulled off his hat and ran fingers through his hair. "You reckon they could've been talking about three other fellows — not us?"

Mungor shrugged. "Possible — but you said they called them some of the James gang. I'm wishing now we'd taken a bit of time before pulling out —"

"Yeh," Larch said. "I was holding some damn good cards when you give me the high sign, and then went busting on by to head off Mungor before he could come in. Don't see why a few more minutes would've hurt."

186

Sonny's shoulders lifted, fell in resignation. "Figured we'd best get the hell out of there fast."

Mungor nodded. "Was smart to play it safe. If there was something to it, it could've cost us our lives."

"Anyway it's done," Larch said. "What's next? We going somewheres special or we just high-tailing it?"

"First off we'll pull in soon's we see a decent place, camp for the night. Horses didn't get much rest back there. Come morning, we'll head south."

"For where?" Sonny asked. He appeared relieved and to have returned to his old self — carefree and interested again in adding to his poke.

"Was aiming to hit Santa Fe, then go on down into the Rio Grande Valley — place called Albuquerque. But just to play it safe — if there is somebody doing some figuring — we'll pass them up, keep going down the river till we get to Socorro."

"Something special about it?"

"Yeh, a fat bank — and the fact it's only three, maybe four days from the Mexican border."

20

Suddenly taut, Mungor drew his horse to a stop. It was midafternoon of a day almost a week after they had ridden out of Las Vegas. They had reached the outskirts of Socorro, separated to enter singly and ostensibly alone as was customary, after which, when the time came to act, they would rejoin. . . . But here was trouble.

Three men, all wearing stars and with leveled rifles, had stepped abruptly from behind a large mound of mesquite and were facing him.

"Hold it right there!" the oldest of the trio — apparently the sheriff — ordered crisply. "And best you put up your hands. Sure would hate to put a bullet in an innocent man."

Mungor raised his arms slowly, studied the lawman narrowly as he advanced toward him. Did they believe him to be alone, or had they seen Sonny and Larch cut off to take different roads into the settlement? He wondered — wondered also if this could be only routine procedure followed by the sheriff and his deputies, or had they been warned to be on the lookout for three outlaws — three members of the "James gang"?

"Where you heading, cowboy?"

The sheriff, a swarthy, somewhat overweight man, a gold chain with a dangling bear's tooth as an ornament looped across his leather vest, had lowered his weapon, was now relying upon his two deputies and their rifles.

"Town right ahead, whatever the hell it's called," Mungor replied, making a show of irritation. "What're you stopping me for? Can't a man ride —"

"Can do without your yapping," the lawman said coldly. "Town's called Socorro. Mighty funny you don't know that."

"Went through a dozen places back up the line, didn't know their names either."

"If you don't know where you are, what do you want here in Socorro?"

"Nothing except to eat, get myself a night's sleep —"

"That mean you're moving on in the morning?"

Mungor shrugged. "Maybe. Just might

like the place, hang around a couple of days. You going to tell me what you're stopping me for?"

"Looking for somebody special," the sheriff said. "You alone?"

Mungor swore, glanced to either side. "You see anybody with me?"

"No, reckon not —"

"Then you could say I'm alone."

"That ain't so, Sheriff!" one of the deputies declared angrily. "I seen three riders top out that hill north of here. He was one of them."

Mungor twisted about, coolly threw his glance to the rise on the trail — a good mile or more distant — brought his attention back to the younger lawman.

"You got mighty good eyes, Deputy," he said, his tone icy, "and I sure don't appreciate being called a liar. You put down that rifle and —"

"Never you mind now," the sheriff cut in. "I reckon Billy could be wrong, it being a far piece to that hill, but it don't call for you to get all riled up. Suppose you just ride on; do your eating and sleeping, and then come sunup, keep on going."

Mungor lowered his arms, settled back on the saddle as relief trickled through him. "Reckon that's just what I'll do, Sheriff.

However, if the rest of the folks in your town ain't no more hospitable than you, could be I won't even stay the night."

"That'd be a mighty big favor," the lawman said indifferently. "I got aplenty to fret over without you hanging around."

Mungor rode on, following the main trail until it came to an intersection. There he turned right, continued on for the plaza around which, he recalled, the business houses were arranged. Reaching the square, he traveled along its south side until he came to a saloon where he drew up at its hitch rack. Dismounting, he glanced about.

Sonny's horse was tied to a post directly opposite. Larch, too, had arrived. Slouched against the front wall of the Red Rock Saloon, hat tipped forward over his eyes, he was evidently dozing in the warm sunlight. The neck of a bottle of whiskey, probably just purchased, was visible in the pocket of his duster.

Duster . . . Mungor swore. He'd cautioned both men about wearing the long coats when they first entered a town where a robbery was planned. Larch had either forgotten or had seen fit to ignore the precaution. One day soon he and the gunman were going to do some settling up, that was for damn sure — and that day likely wasn't far off! Mungor paused in his thoughts, shrugged them off. The hell with Larch. The time when they'd be parting and going their separate ways on the yonder side of the border was near; he reckoned he could put up with the gunman until then.

Pivoting slowly, Mungor, his features slack, let his eyes sweep the plaza. Several elderly men were on the benches in the center of the tree-shaded square; a few others, including two or three women, were moving along the board sidewalks.

He heard a laugh at that moment, recognized it as belonging to Sonny. Shifting his attention, he located the younger man standing in front of another saloon, one termed the Mexican Hat, a girl beside him. Mungor sauntered out into the street and caught his young partner's eye. He shook his head, gestured at a third saloon, a ragtag affair sandwiched in between a drug store and a boot-repair shop.

Crossing to it, Mungor entered, ducking in order to pass under the low doorway of the thick-walled adobe structure. There were no patrons, only a Mexican bartender who stared at him as if surprised his establishment was being favored with business.

"Whiskey," Mungor said, leaning up against the plank counter.

"No, señor — tequila — vino," the man said.

"Tequila," Mungor amended and turned as a shadow darkened the entrance. It was Sonny, with Larch only a breath behind him.

Mungor bucked his head at the Mexican, pointed to his partners. The man behind the counter took up two more fairly large glasses, filled them half full of the clear, fiery liquor, placed them before Sonny and Larch, and shoved a saucer of salt toward them.

"You in a big hurry or something?" Sonny asked. "Was just getting myself acquainted with —"

"Forget that," Mungor cut in quietly and related his encounter with the sheriff and the two deputies at the edge of town. "Don't know for sure what it's all about — but I've got a hunch the word's got here ahead of us again like it did in Las Vegas — to be on the watch for three men."

"Ain't no doubt of it," Larch said morosely, ignoring the tequila and taking a drink from his own bottle. "Expect if you'd take a look in that sheriff's office, you'd find some pretty pictures of us tacked up on the wall. Been plenty of time for them to get some drawed up and passed along."

Sonny downed the tequila, gasped, swallowed hard several times. Larch grinned, passed his bottle to the younger man.

"That Mex stuff ain't much good, is it, kid?" he said and turned to Mungor. "So we best clean out that bank right now — that what you're saying?"

Mungor nodded. "We'll mount up, ride out of the square, and meet behind the bank. Place there where we can leave the horses, then walk around to the door. Quick as we're back to the horses, we'll head west."

Sonny, his breath recovered, signified his understanding. Larch, restoring his bottle to its pocket, jerked a thumb at the bartender.

"What about him? If that there sheriff come along, asking —"

"Doubt if he savvys anything but Mex —"

"I reckon I'll just make sure," the gunman said and, suddenly drawing his pistol, clubbed the man on the side of the head. As he collapsed behind his counter, Larch added, "Now for sure he ain't going to do no talking, leastwise for a spell."

Mungor made no comment. Reaching for a silver dollar, he dropped it on the bar and stepped to the door. Larch was right; it paid to take no chances. Hesitating briefly in the low entrance, he looked back.

"Five minutes — behind the bank. I've

got a bad feeling about this and I want to get done and out of this town fast as we can."

Stooping, he moved out onto the walk, and, careful to show no haste, walked leisurely to his horse, to an observer nothing more than a man coming in off the trail, having himself a drink, and continuing on his way.

Reaching his horse, he mounted, circled the square, and turned down a side street. Once out of view of the plaza, he doubled back, walked his horse quickly to the rear of the bank. A broadly spreading tree grew behind the structure, and, drawing up to it, he swung down. The trunk of the cottonwood was much too large to wrap the lines around, but there was a post, once part of a fence, standing a stride away and he secured his mount to it.

As he finished up and was putting on his duster, Larch and Sonny rode in, coming from opposite directions. Both drew in beside his horse, dismounted, and tied their animals to the post. Sonny removed his long coat from the roll on his saddle, began to don it while Larch, already suitably attired for the occasion, had a swallow from his bottle.

"Same deal as always?" he asked, when all

was ready.

Mungor said, "Same — Sonny at the door, you look after the people while I get the money. Let's move in."

They started along the side of the building, walking at normal stride so as to attract no more than normal attention. Reaching the entrance, they turned in, pulling their bandannas into place as they did.

Over in back of the counter a man swore in sudden fright and exasperation and came to his feet as Larch, gun in hand, bore down on him. Two others — one behind the single teller's cage, the other in an adjoining office — also lunged to their feet but offered no resistance.

Immediately Mungor stepped in to do his part of the operation, now down so pat for each that no time was lost in hesitation or indecision. Seizing a pair of saddlebags that had been draped over the back of a chair in the teller's quarters, Mungor scooped the cash, currency, and coins alike into it, turned quickly to the safe, a small metal affair on wheels that contained many shelves, and relieved it of its packets of currency.

By the time he had emptied the iron box, Larch had herded the two employees into the private office with the third member of the crew, closed the door, and was locking it. Sonny, at the entrance to the building was giving no indication that anything was amiss.

"Ready," Mungor said, coming out from behind the low partition and heading for the door. That bad feeling he'd had earlier was for nothing, he reckoned; the robbery couldn't have gone smoother.

He heard Larch swear as he stumbled against something, but it did not delay the gunman as Mungor could hear the rap of his heels on the bare floor immediately in back of him.

"Nobody's coming," Sonny said, pulling open the thick door and leading the way out onto the walk. "It sure is getting easier and easier to —"

A spatter of gunshots broke the warm hush as bullets thudded into the wall of the bank behind them. Mungor wheeled, crouched as a chain of echoes began to run along the structures lining the square. The sheriff, with his two deputies, had just reached the intersection. By sheer accident they had come upon the robbery.

"Run for it!" Mungor shouted and broke for the rear of the building and their waiting mounts.

Gunshots again ripped through the quiet. Mungor drew his weapon, snapped a shot at the lawmen, coming off their frantically milling horses to drop low in the dusty street. Larch, too, had opened up, and as Mungor turned, he saw one of the deputies go down.

"Larch — what's he doing?" Sonny yelled.

Mungor, not slowing, looked back. The gunman had spun. A stride or two away from him a bottle lay on the ground. Larch's whiskey had fallen from the pocket of his coat and he was attempting to retrieve it.

"No!" Mungor shouted. "Let it go, Larch! Come on!"

The gunman hesitated, glanced toward Mungor, then back to the bottle, shining in the sunlight. In that same moment of time he suddenly stiffened, staggered.

"He's hit!" Sonny said tautly as he and Mungor gained the rear of the bank building.

The horses were only half a dozen strides away. Mungor slowed, looked back up the street. Larch was on his hands and knees, head sagging from his shoulders. His thick body jolted as more bullets slammed into him. He hung there briefly, stubbornly fighting to rise, and then abruptly dropped face down in the loose dirt.

"They got him," Mungor heard Sonny say in a bitter tone as he emptied his pistol at the lawmen. "Them damned badge-toters —"

"Nothing we can do for him," Mungor cut in harshly, as he reached his horse and yanked the lines free of the post. "Come on!"

Sonny was in the saddle as quickly as he, and together they spurred away from the bank and the big cottonwood, rode hard for a row of huts that would hide them from the street.

"They cut him down — them damned, stinking lawmen," Sonny said again as if he couldn't get it off his mind. "They got him —"

Mungor nodded grimly. "Yeh, the law — and a damned bottle of whiskey," he said as they rushed on.

21

Side by side, bent low over their horses, Mungor and Sonny raced down the narrow, alleylike passageway separating twin rows of adobe huts. Dogs were barking frantically, and strained faces peered out at them from windows on both sides.

There were no more gunshots to be heard, and Mungor guessed that the sheriff and his remaining deputy, augmented perhaps by several volunteers, were in the process of getting mounted and starting a pursuit. The few minutes' delay was granting Sonny and him a slight lead.

He looked ahead of his horse. The lane was ending, melting into an open field. Dust now hung behind them in a thick, yellow cloud, but he knew it would not hide them from the posse once it swung into the street. Off to the right a short distance he could see a small house, all but surrounded by fields of corn. At once Mungor veered toward it, trusting that Sonny would note the change in course immediately and follow.

He gained the first of the tall stalks, was aware then that Sonny was still with him although a long stride behind. A man rushed through the open doorway of the house as they pounded by, waving his arms excitedly and yelling something unintelligible. Mungor barely noticed but Sonny shouted an answer which brought on more arm waving and some fist shaking.

They reached the far end of the cornfield. Mungor could neither hear nor see the posse, but he knew the lawman and his supporters could not be far off; the dust churned up by Sonny's horse, and his, marked their route as well as would signs with pointing arrows.

"Which way?" Sonny asked, swiping at the sweat on his face as he rode in alongside.

The tall man pointed toward a spur of trees extending from a row of buttes and bald, dark hills on to the west, and roweled his horse. As the bay he was riding lunged forward and began to gallop across the gently rising ground, Sonny hurried to catch up, and then again together, knee to knee, they rushed to gain cover.

Reaching the small, thin grove, planted at

some time in the past as a break by someone grown weary of the ceaseless winds sweeping in from the plains, Mungor halted. Well hidden in the growth, he sat motionless on his heaving horse, flat eyes fixed on the far corner of the cornfield where the posse should first appear.

Nearby, Sonny had drawn his pistol, was holding it ready in his hand while he awaited the lawman's party.

"Aim to get me that fat sheriff — and that damn deputy, too, if I can," he said, again brushing away the sweat collected on his taut face. "I'll square things up for old Larch —"

Mungor threw an irritated glance at the younger man, eyes pausing briefly on the weapon. "Put it away," he snapped. "You're a fool thinking you owe Larch anything."

"Figured him a friend —"

"Maybe he was, and maybe not. Anyway, he knew what he was doing — knew he was taking a hell of a chance going back for that bottle of whiskey."

Sonny's boyish features were clouded. "Yeh, reckon so, but that sheriff — he could've sung out, let Larch throw down his gun."

"Not how it goes at a time like that," Mungor said, his attention again on the corn-

202

field. The posse should have come into view by then. What was holding it up? "Nobody stops to do any talking — besides, you know how Larch felt about jail. Said he'd never let them lock him up again."

Sonny nodded. "I reckon it was how he'd want it. . . . Sure a waste of a lot of money — what he was carrying, I mean. Wish't now you was still looking after it. We'd had his part to split."

Sonny broke off as Mungor drew to sudden alert. A rider had appeared — not at the end of the cornfield, but farther over where another windbreak had been planted. Shortly, a second horseman came into view — and then three more.

Mungor grinned. His luck was still holding. Not only had he escaped the hail of bullets back in the street when Larch had been cut down, but the posse had guessed wrong, were looking for Sonny and him a considerable distance off in the opposite direction. The drifting clouds of dust had confused them.

"Let's get out of here," he said, turning his horse deeper into the trees. "We'll keep on going west till we can find a town, stay there a couple of days or so, and let things blow over. . . . Could split up if you'd like."

Sonny, keeping up close as they wound

their way through the brush and taller growth, was silent for a long minute, and then shook his head.

"Naw, I'd rather we'd keep on like we are — you and me. We ain't far from the border, you said, so I'm for going on with what we planned."

Mungor's satisfaction showed in the smile that tugged at his lips. "That's how I see it. We're getting close and we might as well stick together and finish it up. Still a couple more towns between here and there that'll be good for a few thousand dollars more."

"Ain't but two of us. It'll be kind of hard —"

"We can manage if we're smart."

"Yeh, reckon that's so. You've been right every time. . . . How much you figure we got back there in that bank?"

"Five or six thousand — not as much as I'd hoped for, but dividing it two ways instead of three, helps."

"Sure does. You know something, Mungor, I had a half notion, when I seen Larch go down, to run back there and get that money-belt thing off him."

The tall man threw a glance over his shoulder. There were no signs of pursuit. Turning back to Sonny he shook his head. "You that anxious to cash in your chips?"

"Nope, sure ain't — not with all the plans I got for living high on the hog in Mexico."

"Expect that's why you didn't do it — something inside stopped you. Was different with Larch. Nothing mattered to him, one way or another. Probably, down deep, he wanted to die."

"Wanted to? That don't —"

"Every now and then you come across men who've turned that way. They've been around death so much that they're hardened to it and life don't mean much. Makes them take chances, long ones that most men back away from. . . . Looks like a sign of some kind on ahead —"

Sonny leaned forward on his saddle, focused his eyes on the faded lettering of a board nailed to a post.

"Sign says Bent Springs thirty miles," he reported. "There's a road, too —"

"Bent Springs," Mungor echoed. "Reckon it'll be our new home for a spell."

Deputy Ben Houston drew up at the rack fronting the Sunnyside Saloon in the settlement along the river and dismounted. He stood for a time in the clean, driving sunlight, glancing about as he dusted himself off with a few halfhearted passes of his open hand, while he wondered exactly where he was. In New Mexico Territory, for sure, and at a saloon called the Sunnyside according to a sign on the front of the building, but there knowledge ended.

He wasn't even certain he was still on the trail of the killers, having headed south after picking up their trail at a livery stable in Las Vegas, on a hunch — one that assured him they were working toward the Mexican border . . . but he could be wrong.

A tight grin cracked his dry lips. He reckoned he'd know shortly; a party traveling south would follow the river and, in so doing, would pass through this village. Winding the lines about the rack's crossbar, Houston crossed to the doorway of the saloon and entered.

Two men, Mexicans or Spaniards, he couldn't tell which, were at the crude bar carrying on an animated conversation while the saloonkeeper, a ruddy-faced German, looked on.

"Whiskey," the lawman ordered when the man moved over to face him.

The drink served, Houston laid a silver dollar on the bar, kept a finger on it as the saloonkeeper started to pick it up.

"Looking for three men," he said as the man, puzzled, glanced up in surprise. "Tall fellow, a kid, and a heavyset gunslinger."

The German stepped back, folded his thick arms across his ample belly. "So?"

Houston reached into his shirt pocket, exhibited his star. "They're killers. Been trailing them all over Kansas, parts of Colorado and Wyoming — now down into New Mexico."

The saloonman shrugged. "They have not been in here, but I did see three riders following the road along the river."

"You get a good look at them?" the deputy asked, tensely.

"Not good, but it was them. I remember the boy. Was several days ago."

Houston sighed with relief. He was still on the right track; they were headed south — undoubtedly for the Mexican border.

"How far to Mexico?" he asked, downing his drink.

The saloonkeeper's thick shoulders rose and fell in a display of uncertainty. "Two hundred-fifty mile, maybe three hundred."

The lawman pointed to the bottle of whiskey, motioned for a refill. It was good whiskey, the best he'd tasted in months.

"Any big towns between there and this place, whatever it's called?"

The saloonman poured the drink, again moved his shoulders. "All are small," he said in his precise, heavily accented voice, "smaller than this place which is called Albuquerque, until you come to Socorro. It is the only town of size."

"How far?"

The German frowned, turned to his other patrons, and voiced a question in Spanish. Coming back around, he said: "It will be eighty mile — down the river. There is also the place called Las Cruces which is farther, but it is close to the border of Mexico."

Houston finished off his drink, his mind now moving swiftly. Picking up his change and thanking the saloonkeeper, he returned to the hitch rack. The killers were getting close to the border — too close, and if ever they crossed over he could call it quits. Somehow he must gain on them, get out in front.

Las Cruces . . . That would be his best bet. Take a chance that they would halt at Socorro, hang around for a few days, perhaps with a plan in mind to rob the bank there before they continued on south to this Las Cruces, the last stop before the border. If he rode hard he should be there ahead of them — waiting.

He'd be gambling on a hunch again, Houston thought with a wry smile, but that's what he'd been forced to do ever since the hunt began. But this time it would be different; he would be putting it all on the line, and either he'd have them — or he'd lose them.

22

Bent Springs consisted of the Antlers Hotel & Restaurant, Crockett's Livery Stable, Loven's General Store, two saloons — the Silver Queen and the Cattleman's; a town marshal with office and jail, a doctor's office, and very little else worthy of note.

It hunched, a small, closely gathered collection of frame and adobe structures, at the foot of a high mountain upon which grew pines, cedars, piñons, and an occasional spruce. Midway up the formation's west slope, a spring burst from the dark soil to course down the steep grade in a noisy, foaming cascade to where it was trapped in a catch basin and thereafter served as a water source for the settlement's pitcher pumps, irrigation ditches, and stock ponds.

Looking down upon the town from the crest of the mountain, Mungor took it all in thoughtfully, noting mentally that it was not only complete insofar as their needs were concerned but, additionally, was well off the usual trails that crisscrossed the country.

Sonny further agreed, at a time later, when they turned into the town's single street and halted at the rack fronting the hotel. A girl appeared in the doorway, stood there briefly, and then stepped out into the open, closing the dust-clogged screen quietly behind her.

Sonny whistled appreciatively. Dark-haired, with large, doelike black eyes, and full lips, she was most attractive in the pale blue dress that fit close and displayed her young, shapely figure.

"Now there's something!" he murmured under his breath.

Mungor, sitting quietly in his saddle, swore, wagged his head at the younger man's sudden interest.

"Best you watch your step here," he warned. "Town's small, and fooling around with her could get you — us — in a lot of trouble. She's probably the daughter of the hotel's owner — she's sure not one of your two-dollar doxies."

"Can sure see that," Sonny said, coming down off the saddle. "I —"

"Just you keep remembering we're here to hide out. You stir up this place against us and we'll like as not never see Mexico."

Sonny, hat off and in one hand, struggling

to smooth his curling hair with the other, nodded impatiently. "Quit worrying about me. I ain't never yet let no woman get me in trouble. I know how to handle them."

Mungor shrugged, dismounted. It had been a hard ride through rough country, and he was tired right down to bone marrow. It would be good to lay over for a few days, and they could if that damn Sonny didn't mess things up with his woman chasing. Hesitating at the rack, Mungor turned his attention to the porch of the Antlers.

Hat still off, Sonny was talking to the girl. She was smiling prettily, a faint blush suffusing her cheeks as she listened. No doubt the younger man was feeding her his string of compliments which always seemed to set him in solid with any woman.

"We get a room in there?" Mungor called, his tone impatient. A few persons along the street had paused, were looking at them in curiosity. The town's lawman would be showing up next, he reckoned.

Sonny, followed by the girl, moved toward him, a wide smile on his face. "This here's Angelina Runnstrom," he said. "Her pa owns the hotel. She says there's aplenty of rooms because there ain't hardly anybody ever comes here 'cepting ranchers living on to the west of us. . . . My pal here's named

Mungor, Angelina."

The girl was even more attractive up close, Mungor saw, as he touched the brim of his hat with a forefinger.

"My pleasure," he murmured and wondered what all Sonny had told her about them. He'd best keep a tight mouth until he could talk with his young partner and learn just who and what they were as well as their intentions.

The room assigned them by Angelina's father, Carl, a towering, thick-chested man with a pronounced limp — a souvenir of his time as a northwoods lumberjack the girl had explained as she escorted them to their quarters — was better than expected. It was clean, airy, and lacked the usual stained and yellowing wallpaper, ragged carpet, and broken-down furniture ordinarily encountered in such places; it would be a good, comfortable place to stay if nothing happened that would force them to move on.

Later in the day after they'd cleaned up, visited the barbershop for a shave, and were on their way back to the hotel, Sonny pointed to the general store.

"Expect I'd best get myself a new shirt — one I got's seen its best days. Goes for these pants, too."

Mungor smiled. "This on account of that

girl? She must be sort've special — I ain't ever seen you do so much sprucing up for a woman before."

Sonny rubbed at his smooth cheeks, stroked his neatly trimmed mustache. The barber, at the younger man's insistence, had been more than generous with lotion, and it would not be difficult for anyone to guess where he had just been.

"Reckon so. She's real different, the kind a man would be willing to tie up with for good. I expect I'm feeling about the same as you did when you first met Darsie."

Mungor's features hardened and his eyes narrowed. "Darsie — what do you know about her?"

Sonny glanced away, swallowed hastily. "Not much — only what Larch said you told him — that she was the prettiest —"

"Don't recollect talking about her."

The younger man swore. "Well — damn it! How'd I know about her being so beautiful and all that if you hadn't told him! You coming with me to the store?"

Mungor shook his head. "What I'm wearing'll do me till we get to Mexico," he said and turned away.

He was still thinking of Darsie and what Sonny had said about her. She had been beautiful — beautiful beyond description, damn her to hell — and remembering her even now was like twisting a knife in an open wound. He wished he could recall what else he'd told Larch about her.

Sonny had reached Loven's, and Mungor, continuing slowly, made his way back to the Antlers. As he mounted the three steps that led to the porch which extended across the building's width, a short, lean man wearing a star rose from one of the chairs Runnstrom had thoughtfully provided for his tenants and advanced toward him.

"Like to do some palavering," the lawman said. "Name's Hitchcock, town marshal."

Mungor halted, folded his arms across his chest, and leaned back against one of the posts supporting the porch roof.

"Glad to know you, Marshal. I'm Dave Mungor."

"Been told. Your partner's called Sonny."

Mungor smiled. The word had gotten around fast, as could be expected.

"Right," he said, "and if you're wanting to know what we're doing here, why, we're just passing through on our way to Texas. Got tired of riding, and not being in no big hurry, we decided to rest up a bit in your town. No law against that, is there?"

"Nope, can't say as there is," Hitchcock replied, shifting his gunbelt. Every loop held a cartridge, Mungor noticed, and the pistol appeared new. "Just that it's my job to know everybody that blows in. We ain't much for strangers. You cowhands?"

Mungor stirred indifferently. "Now and then, all depends on what kind of work we can find."

The lawman pulled off his hat, brushed at the faint shine of sweat on his forehead. "Well, there ain't no work of no kind around here! Can't even keep our own folks busy, so there sure ain't no use of you —"

"Already seen that, Marshal — we're not after anybody's job. All we want's a few days' rest for us and our horses, and we'll move on. That jake with you?"

The lawman's seamy face assumed a more severe expression. "Yeh, reckon it is," he said, pleased at being accorded such deference. "Just don't stir up no trouble."

"Not aiming to," Mungor said, and nodding to the marshal, he crossed the porch and entered the hotel.

He saw but little of Sonny in those next two days, not even at meals or bedtime, the younger man devoting his time exclusively to Angelina. While Mungor in no way resented it — it was good to be alone, do a bit of planning for the future — time not only began to weigh heavily upon him but concern for Sonny and his activities with Angelina had increased.

On several occasions he had become aware of rendezvous in one of the hotel's vacant rooms, and it was apparent that Carl Runnstrom was becoming suspicious of their being constantly together. Sooner or later the man would stumble onto them, and when he did, matters would quickly come to a head — perhaps, end in violence.

At first Mungor decided to stay out of it, simply pull out on his own and let Sonny face the music by himself. But then there was the matter of the bank in Las Cruces — the last holdup that was on his list before reaching the border. He knew he could not manage it alone.

"We're pulling out in the morning — early," he announced bluntly the evening of the fourth day after making a special and successful effort to intercept the younger man.

Sonny frowned and then, after a moment, said, "Suits me."

Mungor looked closely at his partner. "What about the girl? You been —"

"Aim to marry her," Sonny cut in blandly and, as Mungor drew up in surprise, added: "Won't be right away. Figure to come back for her soon's I get settled on the other side of the border."

Mungor relaxed slightly. "She agree to that?"

"Yeh — more or less. Didn't take too kindly to the idea at first. Said she wanted to come along with me now, but I told her we had to go to Las Cruces on some real important business and she'd best wait here. Only thing, she ain't looking for us to leave for a spell."

"Well, you tell her tonight that we'll be gone in the morning," Mungor said and then, eyes narrowing, said, "You talk much to her about us — about where we've been and where we're going, and such?"

"Well, some of it. Man tells things like that to his woman — just about has to when they get to asking questions."

Mungor swore quietly. "Like as not you've said too much — but you be damn sure you don't say anything about us going to Mexico. Trying to keep our whereabouts quiet, and with her passing things along like she already has, that lawman — if we've got one trailing us — will mighty soon get wind of us."

"Hell, there ain't nobody dogging us. They'd've met up with us by now. Wouldn't make no difference, anyways — us being so close to the border. Time he got the word and could make it to here, we'll be in Mexico."

"Maybe," Mungor said, forced to admit the truth and logic of the younger man's statement. "Now, I'll be pulling out at first light. You be ready to ride if you're going."

"Can bank on it," Sonny assured him and glanced up.

Angelina, fetching in an embroidered pink shirtwaist, cord riding skirt, boots, and with a gun belt around her small middle was standing in the archway that separated the restaurant from the hotel's lobby. He grinned at her, got to his feet.

"We're going out and do some shooting," he said to Mungor. "Angie's real good at it — can ride, too."

The tall man smiled, nodded. "I'll bet she is. . . . Don't forget about the morning."

"I won't," Sonny replied lightly. "I'll be there.

23

The bank at Las Cruces was unusually well guarded. Mungor, with Sonny at his side, stood in the shade of a small tree near the hotel where they were staying and considered the squat, glass-fronted structure. It was the third day after their arrival, and constant surveillance on the part of Mungor had failed to determine a safe time at which they could move in and carry out their plans. Two armed guards were in evidence at all times.

"Kind of like maybe they been expecting us," Sonny observed.

The identical thought had occurred to Mungor, but how could it be true? Discounting Angelina who could hardly have accidentally leaked the information to anyone in time, who would know they intended to be in that particular settlement at that specific time? It had been days now since Socorro and their last brush with the law — and, too, they had not continued southward after the incident as they could have been expected to do; instead they had pulled off the main roads and trails and holed-up in a quiet, out-of-the-way settlement buried in the hills, where they had been the only passersby in weeks.

"We best forget it," he said after a time. "There's something haywire — and we'd never get out of there alive if we tried it."

Sonny nodded soberly. "For sure. Money don't do a man no good when he's dead. We got enough for Mexico, anyway."

Mungor would have felt better about it if they could have increased their pokes by another three or four thousand dollars; twenty thousand each would have been a nice round figure to start life with on the other side of the border, but it wasn't to be apparently, and since he was now so near to realizing his goal, it would be foolish to press his luck even if he still enjoyed the privileges of a charmed life.

"Expect we'd as well move on," he said, brushing at the sweat misting his eyes, and coming about. "Not but a short ride to Mexico if we take what they call the Border Trail. Can leave here around dark, after it cools off a bit, be over there by sunup."

Sonny smiled happily. "Suits me. I got a

221

little Mex gal waiting back at the hotel — but I'll be ready."

Mungor looked closely at the younger man as they walked slowly toward the inn. "What about Angelina? Thought you was all set to marry her —"

Sonny shrugged. "This ain't got nothing to do with her — or hitching up with her. This here's nothing but some fun."

"You still going back for her — like you promised?"

"Maybe so — maybe not. Things are kind of different now that she ain't around."

Mungor, aware of an uneasiness growing steadily within him, coupled with an urge to move on immediately and get across the border, scrubbed at his jaw nervously and glanced off into the south — and Mexico.

"Just maybe I'll take the notion to head out sooner, not wait for dark. You be ready if I do?"

Sonny nodded. "Ain't no problem. Give me an hour to take care of the little Mex and I'll be rearing to go."

Mungor gave that a few moments' thought, and then said: "Can do it this way. I'll pick up our gear, go down to the stable and saddle up the horses, get set to ride. When I'm done with that, I'll come by the hotel for you. What's your lady friend's

222

room number?"

"Nine — door at the end of the hall on the second floor. . . . Sure take it as a big favor. I just can't pass up that little Mex!"

Mungor only shrugged. "I'll be there in one hour," he said and walked on.

It took less time than he had anticipated, or else the persistent feeling that all was not exactly as it should be hurried his movements. But he had told Sonny he'd give him an hour and he'd stick by it, and thus with a few minutes to pass he left the livery barn and sought out the nearest saloon. There in the cool dimness he treated himself not to whiskey but several beers, since the day was hot, and mulled over things as they were.

His long, careful planning had worked out fairly well; to be sure he'd lost Larch — but he'd expected that more or less, and the robberies of the Bonanza casino at Las Vegas and the banks at Hays City and Las Cruces had all misfired, but those failures could hardly be laid at his door; the planning had been perfect — matters had gone awry by accident. But he could forget all that now. He was near the end of the rainbow, and he reckoned he had accomplished what he'd set out to do — collect the fortune that he felt was due him from an ungrateful world. All that remained now was to make the short, forty-mile or so ride to the border, cross over, and start enjoying the good life.

Mungor stirred, glanced through the open doorway. Sonny's hour was up, he guessed, and rising, he went back to the stable, got the horses, and, habitually cautious, left the structure by its rear door, circled, and came into the hotel from its back as well. Tying the animals to the rack, Mungor climbed the few steps that led up to the landing, opened the door, and entered. He halted immediately.

A dozen or more men were gathered there, blocking the narrow passageway. Two of them wore stars and one, evidently the sheriff, was talking to a woman standing beyond his view inside the room. Tension lifted suddenly in Mungor. He glanced at the number on the door: Nine. It was the Mexican girl's quarters.

Taut, wary, Mungor worked his way quietly into the crowd. He saw then the prostrate figure of a man, half in half out of the doorway, but only the legs were visible. It was enough; the familiar boots, the new pants so recently purchased in Bent Springs — it could only be Sonny. A hard smile cracked Mungor's lips; Sonny's craving for women had finally caught up with him!

Pulling back, the tall man started to retrace his steps to the stairs, froze as the man next to him turned.

"That big-eyed little gal sure filled that fellow full of lead! Shot him five times —"

A frown knotted Mungor's brow. Big-eyed — could he mean Angelina? Curiosity aroused, he glanced about. No one was paying any attention to him, their interest being centered on the lawman and the person to whom he was speaking inside the room.

"What happened?"

The man came around quickly, eyes bright, anxious to relate what he knew. "Fellow there had himself one too many gals, seems. Was visiting the little Mexican señorita when Big-eyes showed up and caught him at it."

"Who is she?" Mungor asked, certain he knew.

"Ain't heard no name, only that she come from over in the Black Mountain Country. Told Herkenhoff — he's the sheriff — that the dead man was supposed to marry her."

"I see."

Angelina apparently had decided not to wait for Sonny's return, had instead followed either on her own horse or by stagecoach, and arrived sometime that morning. Likely she had asked at the hotel's desk for

Sonny, had been directed to his room —
and encountered him either going into or
coming from the Mexican girl's quarters.

"Anybody know who he is?"

Mungor knew he was now pushing his
luck, hanging around, but it was important
to have a full understanding of the situation
and how much, if any, the law knew about
him.

"Was called Sonny. Was a big-time outlaw.
Heard Arnie Boyle — he's one of Herkenhoff's deputies — tell Pete Spencer — he's
the other'n, that this bird and a couple of
partners raised all kinds of hell up in Kansas
and Wyoming, shooting and killing and robbing banks.

"And Herkenhoff's sure it's the same
bunch that cleaned out the bank in Socorro
not long ago — shot one of the deputies,
but they got one of them while they was
making a run for it. Sheriff sent Spencer to
get some lawman from Colorado that's been
hanging around here for a few days. Seems
he's been trailing them ever since they killed
a homesteader up around Denver. Herkenhoff figures this here Colorado lawman can
say for sure whether Sonny's one of them
or not."

Mungor nodded slowly. He'd been right
— there was a lawman dogging their tracks

— and he was there in town at that very moment having figured what plan they were following, gotten ahead, and settled down to wait for them to ride in and make a move. Whoever he was, he'd be able to identify Sonny, and then the word would go out for him. But he'd have the jump on them — he'd be gone.

"Don't recollect seeing you around here before —"

Tension was gripping Mungor tightly but he forced an offhand smile. "Can say the same for you! Truth is, I just come in from over Arizona way — Tucson. Only been around a couple of days."

"Reckon that explains it," the man said. "Well, expect I'd best get back to my business —"

"Goes for me, too —"

"What kind of business you in?"

"Horses," Mungor said. "Buy up stock for ranchers."

He had turned away, was moving toward the rear entrance to the hotel, and scarcely heard the final words of his talkative, new friend.

"Good luck —"

Mungor glanced back, said, "Same to you," and opening the door, stepped out onto the landing.

He paused there, narrowed eyes searching for anyone suspicious lurking close by. The area was deserted, and descending the steps quickly, he crossed to his horse, swung up into the saddle, and, wheeling, headed south out of town. . . . His luck still held — just as he had known it would. Of the three of them, Larch and Sonny were dead — only he was alive.

24

Ben Houston, sitting at a table in the Amador Inn, penning a letter to his superior in Denver, came to his feet hurriedly upon hearing the message Herkenhoff's deputy, Pete Spencer, relayed to him.

"You're sure it's the kid — Sonny?"

"What we figure. Sheriff wants you to say for sure. Woman killed him."

"What about his partner — Mungor?" Houston pressed anxiously.

"Well, I reckon he's around somewhere — if this here's your man. Woman said the two of them come here together."

Houston picked up the sheaf of papers upon which he had begun his letter — a report, actually — of his search for the three killers. He intended to note that one was now dead, that he believed the remaining two would soon show there in Las Cruces as he was convinced they were working their way to the border — and that he intended to intercept them. Wadding the paper into a ball, he threw it into a coal scuttle standing beside the potbellied heater provided by the inn for winter use and followed Spencer out into the street to the hotel.

It was Sonny. Staring down at the slack, boyish face, Houston smiled in grim satisfaction. There was now only Mungor, the head man, the leader of the killers, to contend with. The law in Socorro had settled with Larch, the gunslinger, downing him with half a dozen slugs: a woman had caught up with Sonny and paid him off in full for whatever crime he had committed against her — and that left Mungor to him. Moving back out of the crowd still gathered in the hallway where the outlaw had fallen, Houston beckoned to Spencer.

"Mungor's smart," he said. "Can bet he's already on his way to the border — or soon will be. I need a fast horse so's I can head him off."

"Can use my sorrel," the deputy said. "He's plenty fast and needs working. I ain't rode him in a week."

"Obliged," Houston said, urgency now beginning to grip him. Each passing moment, he realized, was critical. "Where'll I find him?"

"Down at Jase McIntyre's livery stable,"

Spencer replied. "I'll take you there."

Less than a half hour later Ben Houston, astride the deputy's long-legged gelding, was pounding the road south out of the settlement that led to El Paso. But Mungor would not be heading for the pass city, Spencer had declared; there were too many lawmen on duty there, not to mention the soldiers from the nearby fort who did constant patrol duty.

No, he would cut off the main road a distance below Las Cruces, ford the Rio Grande at a village called Vado most likely, and there follow a seldom-used route known as the Border Trail.

Do the same, Spencer had advised, but when he came to the lava beds — assuming Mungor was ahead of him — forget the Trail, swing across the embankment of black, jagged rock and bear to the right.

The outlaw, no doubt, had some knowledge of the country if he had made plans previously and would stay on the Trail. Houston, by chancing the lava formation, could cut off a good five miles and that should put him out in front of Mungor — or at least in sight of him. If it proved to be the former, all well and good; it would simply be a matter of waiting, letting the outlaw come to him. If it turned out to be the latter, then it would be a race to see who could reach the border first.

Spencer had been right. Hours later, Houston, letting the tireless sorrel have his way after guiding him carefully across the dangerous volcanic field, caught sight of a lone rider well in the distance to the west.

Immediately, tension and elation rising as one within him, he drew his telescope from his saddlebags, extended it fully, and trained it on the vague figure. He could not be certain; he thought the man fit the description given him of Mungor, but at such long range, even with his glass, he could not say definitely that it was the outlaw.

But, logically, it was. A rider, alone, moving fast in the direction of the border, that added up to Mungor. The lawman closed the brass tube, returned it to its place. He had no choice but to chance it, to assume that the rider was the killer.

Houston swore feelingly, wiped at the sweat on his face, and spurred the sorrel to a faster gait. Everything had been a gamble — right from the start! He'd been forced to guess, depend on hunches, assume and figure, logically, what the outlaws would do. Each time, fortunately, it had worked out that he was right. He could only hope that he would be right once more.

The rider noticed him a time later, slowed, and then perceptibly increased his pace. Houston, keeping the big sorrel at a steady lope, drew his glass, again had a searching look. He felt sure now that it was Mungor — a lean, square-shouldered man forking a bay horse. That tallied with the descriptions he'd been given of the outlaw as he'd trailed him from place to place, and with that of the stable owner in Las Cruces who stated that the man was riding a bay.

He'd waste no more time on speculation, simply assume it was Mungor and close in, and since he had no idea how near they were to the Mexican border — it was not too far now, he judged — he'd do it as fast as possible. Bending low over the saddle, the lawman called on the sorrel for more speed.

The big horse responded and the gap between the deputy and the outlaw began to shrink. It was now a matter of horseflesh, Houston realized — the sorrel matched against the bay, and each with certain advantages. The sorrel was in excellent condition after days of idleness and rest and was anxious to run; the bay, worn from hours on the trail but by the same token toughened by such, had a head start, needed only to maintain the stretch of sandy flat that lay between them.

Again mopping at the sweat blanketing his face, Houston gauged the distance that separated him from Mungor. The outlaw was now fully aware of the situation and had put his horse to a dead run. The border could not be far, the deputy reckoned, else Mungor would not be pushing his mount so hard.

The gap was finally beginning to narrow, he saw, but the sorrel, red hide shining wetly in the bright sunlight, was now sucking hard for wind. Despite his great strength, the pace he'd maintained across the loose sand had taken its toll. Whether he would have enough left in him to finish the job was problematical.

Houston drew his pistol, cursing the fact that there was no rifle in the boot of Spencer's saddle. Allowing for distance, he aimed at Mungor, pressed off a shot. The bullet fell short. At once the outlaw brought up his weapon, triggered an answer, also futile, and settled lower over the straining bay.

Abruptly the horse faltered, began to break stride. In the next instant he went down, flailing hoofs churning up a cloud of thick, yellow dust. Houston, coming on fast, veered the sorrel hard right. He could not see Mungor, but he knew the killer was somewhere in the dense haze, pistol up and ready to blast him out of the saddle.

A curse ripped from Mungor's lips as the bay went down under him. He had expected it, knowing the horse had given his best, was running that last mile or so on sheer guts, but he had hoped the animal would last until they reached the border — now only a mile or so in the distance.

But it hadn't worked out that way. Luck, for the first time, had dealt him a bad hand. He hit the ground clear of the bay's hoofs and bounded upright in the center of the boiling dust.

He could barely see the lawman, whoever the hell he was, rushing up fast. A hard grin split Mungor's mouth. He still had the upper hand. The fool badge-toter was riding straight into the muzzle of his pistol!

The dust haze cleared. Mungor lunged forward, pistol up and firing. The lawman had cut away, but he got a glimpse of his set face, saw him flinch as a bullet caught him.

And then he felt the numbing shock of lead slugs smashing into his body. He stumbled, allowed his weapon, suddenly very heavy, to lower. He'd been hit bad. Puzzled, he considered that with fading senses. It shouldn't have happened. There was something wrong — he was the one with the charmed life! He'd gone through the war, weathered a dozen shootouts — the man no bullet would ever touch!

But it had happened. He was hit, was dying. The charm had failed him, and it was all over. Mungor realized that with his last conscious thoughts as he stared up at the lawman standing over him.

ABOUT THE AUTHOR

Ray Hogan is an author who has inspired a loyal following over the years since he published his first Western novel *Ex-marshal* in 1956. Hogan was born in Willow Springs, Missouri, where his father was town marshal. At five the Hogan family moved to Albuquerque where Ray Hogan still lives in the foothills of the Sandia and Manzano mountains. His father was on the Albuquerque police force and, in later years, owned the Overland Hotel. It was while listening to his father and other old-timers tell tales from the past that Ray was inspired to recast these tales in fiction. From the beginning he did exhaustive research into the history and the people of the Old West and the walls of his study are lined with various firearms, spurs, pictures, books, and memorabilia, about all of which he can talk in dramatic detail. Among his most popular works are the series of books about Shawn Starbuck, a searcher in a quest for a lost brother, who has a clear sense of right and wrong and who is willing to stand up and be counted when it is a question of fairness or justice. His other major series is about lawman John Rye whose reputation has earned him the sobriquet "The Doomsday Marshal." "I've attempted to capture the courage and bravery of those men and women that lived out West and the dangers and problems they had to overcome," Hogan once remarked. If his lawmen protagonists seem sometimes larger than life, it is because they are men of integrity, heroes who through grit of character and common sense are able to overcome the obstacles they encounter despite often overwhelming odds. This same grit of character can also be found in Hogan's heroines and, in *The Vengeance of Fortuna West,* Hogan wrote a gripping and totally believable account of a woman who takes up the badge and tracks the men who killed her lawman husband by ambush. No less intriguing in her way is Nellie Dupray, convicted of rustling in *The Glory Trail.* Above all, what is most impressive about Hogan's Western novels is the consistent quality with which each is crafted, the compelling depth of his characters, and his ability to juxtapose the complexities of human conflict into narratives always as intensely interesting as they are emotionally involving. His latest novel is *Soldier in Buckskin.*